Sacrifice

A Gryphon Series Novel

By Stacey Rourke

Copyright 2012
Published by Anchor Group Publishing
PO Box 551
Flushing, MI 48433
Anchorgrouppublishing.com
Edited by Melissa Ringsted

Acknowledgements

Thank you to my family and friends for your unwavering support. To the crew of Anchor Group Publishing, thank you for believing in me and motivating me without fail. A big thanks to my amazing editor, Melissa Ringsted, and all of my beta readers. I appreciate you more than you can imagine. And, of course, to the Condu-nuts, you keep reading 'em, I'll keep writing 'em!

Dedicated to my mom and David, thank you for dragging a reluctant teenage me to the gorgeous Biltmore Estate. If it wasn't for you Gabe and Alaina probably would've gotten married on a river boat.

Part One

CHAPTER ONE

"Right jab. Left jab."

My fists connected with the punching bag in time to the commands.

"Right hook. Left hook. No!" Bernard pointed his cane and electricity jolted through me. My muscles seized up, the world swam out of focus, and I could taste metal. "You're being lazy! Again. Left hook."

I used to have an irrational fear of garden gnomes. Then I met one. Turns out it wasn't so irrational. They're evil little jerks. Okay, that's generalizing. Maybe it wasn't all gnomes, just Bernard. In his defense, we didn't really start our relationship off on the right foot. I have what you may refer to as "gnome-phobia". They creep me right out. Therefore, when one walked into my bedroom after being introduced as my Spirit Guide, I had a slight case of the wiggens—by which I mean I screamed my fool head off and whipped every piece of my bedding *and* my sister's at him. The low point came the moment I picked up my sister's stuffed zebra. The second it went airborne things seemed to happen in slow motion.

Kendall screamed, "Mr. Hoofington! Nnnooooooo!"

Bernard got knocked clear across the hall when the dopey, grinning zebra walloped him.

In retrospect it probably wasn't the best way to meet my new mentor. No wonder he got slaphappy with his zappy cane during our training sessions.

With still blurred vision, I swung blindly at the punching bag, missed, spun myself around and landed on the ground tangled in my own legs.

Bernard shuffled over, his cane clicking across the cement floor. Red pointed hat, long white beard, green shirt belted around his paunchy mid-section, and tan pants tucked into tiny little leather boots. Somewhere there was a flower bed with a Bernard-sized hole in it. He leaned against his cane and eyed me with contempt as he crammed one pudgy little hand into the satchel that hung around his waist. Extracting a handful of berries, he popped them into his mouth one after the other. They were fermented. He had a bit of an addiction.

Blue juice dribbled down his white beard as he chomped. "You're not even trying. Such lack of effort by the Conduit is disgraceful."

"Shouldn't you be making cookies in a tree somewhere?" I grumbled under my breath.

"What was that?" He glared. The berries made him especially surly.

I tightened my ponytail and rose to my feet. "I said, 'I'm sorry. Let's go again'," I lied with my best fake grin.

With a brisk nod, Bernard turned on his heel and marched back over to the perimeter of the musty garage. I fought the urge to quicken his trip by punting him there. Our training sessions normally took place at a clearing in the Appalachian Mountains, just outside of the tiny town of Gainesboro, Tennessee where we live. But a couple of weeks ago we got two feet of snow dumped on us. Grams didn't want our warrior alter egos to get lax, so she transformed her one car garage into a training facility. It wasn't much—a punching bag, space heater, and a small area the size of a mid-sized SUV for sparring—but it beat getting frost bitten toes.

I shook out my limbs and awaited Bernard's next command. He banged his tiny cane against the floor to signal it was time to begin. I centered myself and let the power course through me. A smile curled my lips at the surging energy that electrified every muscle and joint of my body.

"Right jab." Dust flew as my fist connected with its target.

"Left jab." The bag rattled on its chain.

"Right hook." Mid-swing a titter of laughter distracted me. Instead of hitting the bag, I caught it and steadied it.

"Remind me again why Kendall doesn't have to train?" I stared daggers at my little sister. She sat huddled on the floor next to the space heater with Alaina, our ex-Spirit Guide.

At the mention of her name Keni's head snapped up. Blonde hair, blue eyes, and the body of a dancer. Females everywhere would hate her if she weren't a genuine sweetheart.

With a smile right out of a toothpaste commercial she beamed. "Because I don't fight." She leaned forward and let one ivory wing slide out of her back. Her feathers were impenetrable and had the ability to heal. A fact I relied on, and occasionally exploited, to keep me alive. "I protect."

"Then why are you here?" I countered.

A flash of hurt shadowed her flawless features. "Moral support. So you don't have to be out here in the dirty, dusty garage alone. Duh."

"Conduit, back to work," Bernard interjected.

I chose to ignore the angry little troll. "And swooning over bridal magazines is your idea of support?"

Alaina looked up guiltily. "That would be my fault."

She pushed a wavy lock of auburn hair behind her ear. For a chick well over three hundred years old, she didn't look a day over twenty-three. I assumed that—along with her pin-up model curves—is what drew my brother, Gabe, to her. Unfortunately, their relationship broke a lot of rules adhered to by The Council. (I have limited knowledge of them. To me they're a group of snobs sent to make the lives of the warriors that fight for them

3

miserable and they are *astounding* at that.) Because of her relationship with Gabe, Alaina got fired as our guide to all things mystical and her humanity was returned to her. She didn't take this well. For weeks she wore nothing except her boyfriend's sweats, refused to leave the couch, and ate ice cream by the gallon. I want to think it was love that prompted my brother to propose to her right around that time, and not his desire to get his sweetheart back into a regular bathing routine, but I can't say for sure. Whatever his motivation, she said yes. He slipped that pretty little rock on her finger, her funk instantly vanished, and our house turned into Wedding Central.

Alaina flipped through the pages of her bridal magazine. "We're searching for just the right dresses and I'm afraid it isn't going well. Kendall agreed to loan me her knowledge of fashion to make sure everything turns out right."

"Conduit," Bernard tried again, his tone tight with irritation.

I cringed and smacked my head against the punching bag. "You're gonna make me wear pink, aren't you?"

Kendall's face went blank, her eyes wide. "Of course!"

"Ugh."

"You don't get to ugh." Kendall jabbed a finger in my direction and her lower lip protruded slightly. "You have a date for the wedding. Ugh's are reserved for those of us that have to go stag because our boyfriend hit a growth spurt, became the star of the lacrosse team, and cheated on us with that skank Sydney Taylor."

I pushed off the bag, cocked my head to the side, and raised both eyebrows.

Keni's face crumbled. "Fine, she's not a skank. I'm sure she's a lovely person. A lovely person that made out with Keith during the Homecoming game while I was on the 50 yard line being crowned Queen."

I couldn't help but chuckle. Part of my sister's calling is a creature of love. All her powers and abilities are derived from the unlimited supply of warmth and goodness that bubbles through her. That makes it practically impossible for her to say anything mean or off color about anyone, even when she *really* wants to.

Our conversation was interrupted when an electric shock struck my left ankle and caused my leg to give out. I squealed and crumbled down on one knee.

"*Conduit!*" Bernard bellowed, his torturous cane still aimed my way. "Can you at least *pretend* that your calling is important to you? Perhaps *attempt* to take this seriously? Your lack of discipline is appalling."

I ground my teeth together and tried to remember what my mom said about respecting elders. For the life of me I couldn't recall it right then …

"We're in the garage and I'm fighting a bag on a chain." My nostrils flared and I fought to steady my breathing. "I'm sorry I don't take that as seriously as you'd like. Put an actual demon in front of me and you wouldn't doubt my dedication for a second."

Bad time for the side door of the garage to open and my half-demon boyfriend to saunter in, trailed by my brother. Bernard's jaw set and his bushy white eyebrows drew together. He never made any attempts to hide his distaste for my beau.

"Except for that one," I tagged on. I tried to sound sorry. Really, I did. But the rush of adrenaline I got whenever I saw the raven-haired Irishman put an audible smile in my voice.

Caleb. Tall, dark, handsome, and all mine. We'd been together for a few months, but the swoon factor of his unbelievable hotness had yet to wear off. I sincerely doubted it ever would. Hints of blue reflected in his glossy ebony locks. He possessed the chiseled jaw of a Greek god, and a slight crook in his nose that added a flaw of humanity to his otherwise untouchable perfection. What he saw in me I had no idea. But all he had to do was give me "that look" and any intelligent thought I had was replaced with incoherent ramblings of *humhna-humhna-humhna.*

I rose to my feet. Everything and everyone disappeared around us. He walked toward me, the glint in those beautiful emerald eyes bordering on mischievous. His lips curled into a knowing grin as he slipped one hand around to the small of my back and pulled me in for a quick kiss.

Kendall noisily turned the pages of her magazine. "Hi, I'm Celeste. I have a boyfriend and I rub it in people's faces even when I know they just got dumped."

Reluctantly I pulled away from Caleb to glare at Keni. "First of all, that whiny voice sounds nothing like me. Secondly, you didn't get dumped. He cheated on you. Big difference."

For a moment she just stared. "Thank you so much for pointing that out. I feel *much* better now."

"You're welcome." I gave her my biggest, most cheerful grin. That threw her pout into overdrive.

Caleb tugged at the bottom hem of my t-shirt, his subtle signal for me to give my sis a break. Fine by me, I'd rather focus on him anyway.

Knowing I had limited time before Bernard got annoyed and shock-happy again, I gave Caleb another quick kiss then whispered for his ears only, "Any luck?"

Regret shadowed his face. "No. Sorry, lovey. He's gone deep underground. I'll keep lookin', but I don't think we're gonna find him until he wants tah be found."

In his spare time, Caleb had been scouring every corner of the earth for traces of my friend, Alec. Something demonic had a hold of poor Alec although we had no idea what, how, or why. Somehow, this decidedly evil Alec had figured out a way to make demonic playthings out of innocent people for his own enjoyment. Before I could figure out a way to stop him, he vanished without a trace.

I hid my disappointment behind a tight-lipped smile. "Thanks for trying."

Caleb hooked his finger under my chin and tipped my head up. "I won't give up. I promise."

I nodded, but said nothing.

Bernard banged his cane against the floor in six rapid-fire successions. His round face flushed red, then purple. "Training time isn't over!"

Caleb glanced over his shoulder at the glowering gnome. "What's with the hostile envir'ment?"

"Oh you know, same old, same old. I don't respect my sacred duty of pummeling inanimate objects, blah, blah, blah. Maybe Gabe will train with me to appease Mr. Sunshine." I looked to my brother with a hopeful expectation.

Bernard folded his arms over his chest and scowled.

"Sorry, Cee," Gabe raked a hand through his recently grown-out hair. He usually kept it buzzed, but Alaina insisted he grow it out for the wedding. He fiddled with the whole inch of it almost as much as Kendall did with hers. The two of them had daily scuffles over 'mirror time' in the bathroom. My low maintenance ponytail and I were very amused by this.

"I don't need to train," he said with a cocky smirk. "I'm a lion. It doesn't get any more badass than that."

Gabe ignored my eye-roll and circled his hands around Alaina's slender wrists to pull her into his waiting arms. She giggled and wrapped her arms around his neck.

"Couples suck," Kendall grumbled and tossed the bridal magazine aside.

Against the far wall of the garage—flanked by Gram's flamingo lawn ornaments—Bernard's pinched up red face warned of an impending gnome-sized embolism.

Just as he opened his mouth to unleash what was sure to be a nasty verbal bashing, Caleb intervened, "I'll spar with her."

Bernard's beady eyes narrowed. "I don't know … "

"I think it's a heck of a lot more effective than me fighting a bag." I matched Bernard's arm fold and raised him a challenging sneer.

Bernard took a deep breath in through his nose, and let it out through pursed lips. "Fine. Do *not* hold back," he barked at Caleb, then pointedly turned his glare to me, "*at all.*"

"Wouldn't dream of it," Caleb shot me a wink.

Gabe unchained the punching bag and leaned it against Grandpa's dusty old work bench, then took a seat on the floor with Alaina and Kendall. Caleb and I faced off in the center of the garage. He yanked off his hooded sweatshirt and tossed it to his sister (That would be Alaina, by the way. Long story. He was abducted by a demonic army as a child and she joined the good guys as a Spirit Guide. Huh, look at that. I made a long story surprisingly short.)

He brought his hands up and struck a defensive pose. The thin material of his white t-shirt tightened across the sculpted muscles of his torso. That visual stimuli caused a wandering gaze that couldn't be helped. With his knees slightly bent, his jeans hugged his thighs in a way that proved very distracting.

"*Ahem* … I'm up here, lovey. Not that I don't appreciate a good oglin'."

I hurriedly assumed a fighting stance, my cheeks and ears burning bright red. "Sorry. I'm good. Let's do it. *This*! Let's do *this*!" Gabe, Alaina, and Kendall all snickered from the sidelines. "Crap. Let's just get this over with."

Caleb's handsome face folded in mock hurt. "Ya say it like that and I'm inclined tah think ya won't enjoy it at all."

"I think we both know that's not true." I grinned.

"Well then…" He jerked his head to the side to crack his neck and blinked hard. When his eyes opened the green was gone. In its place blazed brilliant red irises. Visible red flames danced beneath the surface of his skin. "Give us a kiss."

I leapt forward and spun. My fist raised on a collision course with his throat. He caught my wrist and pinned it behind my back. I winced as my skin sizzled and blistered under his touch.

His breath tickled my ear. "Ya'r gonna have tah do better than that, lovey."

He released me, and I backed away rubbing my charred wrist. That little move had awakened my inner warrior ... and she was ticked. I brought my hands up and beckoned him to advance. "Again."

He came at me fast. A mad flurry of blows and punches. Not one landed. I blocked every swing, countered every jab. We matched blow for blow until the sweat flowed and our damp clothing clung to us like a second skin. I answered an effective uppercut with a downward block and then utilized the split second it took Caleb to regroup to spin into a roundhouse kick. My foot connected with enough force to send him flying backward. He slammed into the metal garage door that twanged and rattled its disapproval. Our audience—except for Bernard— golf-clapped at my victory.

"Well done, well done." Bernard nodded and crammed another handful of berries into his mouth. He eyes had turned glassy. It wouldn't be long before he'd be confessing his undying love to one of Kendall's old Barbie dolls that Grams kept boxed up out here ... *again*. "Now why couldn't you do that earlier? When *I* asked you to?"

I shrugged one shoulder and wiped the sweat from my brow with the back of my hand. "'Cause he's hot."

Bernard stamped his cane against the ground, "Of all the vain, juvenile excuses! His physical attractiveness should have nothing ... "

I held up my hands to calm the angry little man who was, quite literally, spitting mad. "Whoa, whoa, whoa! He's got Titan blood in himself, remember? He can control the elements, and he called fire to him. His hands were scalding hot. That was great motivation to *not get hit!*"

Bernard paused his rant to consider Caleb, who had pulled himself up off the ground and was straightening his jeans that had gotten twisted around his work-boots. For the first time ever, a glimmer of genuine appreciation broke through Bernard's icy façade toward my demonic fella.

"That was actually quite clever," Bernard begrudgingly admitted. "Well done."

"Thank ya," Caleb stood up and ran his fingers through his sweat-dampened locks. "Did it perhaps earn a free pass for our fated Chosen One?"

Just as quickly as the newfound appreciation came on, it vanished and Bernard's go-to scowl returned. "Free pass? What does that mean? Allowing her to run the streets like a hooligan?"

Caleb struggled to suppress the grin that tugged at the corners of his heart-shaped lips. "Nothin' like that, I assure ya. Just an evenin' off to allow the lovely Celeste a chance to recharge her batteries. Any and all attempts at hooligan runnin' will be thwarted. Ya have my word."

This was so completely unexpected and unheard of with Bernard's strict training regime that I crossed my fingers behind my back at the prospect of him actually agreeing to it.

Bernard shook the last of his berries from the satchel onto his palm and mashed them in his mouth. He'd started to sway, and leaned heavily on his cane to remain upright. "Fine, the night is yours. *One* night off. That's it. Tomorrow you train and patrol without complaint."

"Agreed!" I clapped my hands and bounced on the balls of my feet.

"Hey, does that go for us, too?" Gabe asked. "We don't have to patrol tonight?"

Bernard waved one hand in the air. "All of you! One night off. But that's it!" He didn't bother with any further pleasantries. Two raps of his cane against the ground and he vanished into thin air. No doubt heading off to replenish his berry supply (or abduct a Barbie).

Gabe jumped off the ground in one fluid, cat-like motion. "Don't have to tell me twice!" He extended his hands to Keni and Alaina, and yanked them both off the cold cement floor. "I'm thinking pizza and watching the game on TV. What do you say, babe?"

Alaina's moss-green eyes glimmered with excitement. "I've got a better idea! I recorded a marathon of *A Wedding Story* on TLC. We can watch it and take notes on things we like!"

"That *is* even better." Gabe's broad shoulders sagged, but he did his best to feign enthusiasm. "Can we at least order a pizza?"

Kendall raised her hand. "I vote 'yes' to pizza. Grams is staying at Dr. Allyn's again and we have limited food options. It's pizza or week old Chinese."

"Pizza it is," Gabe declared and ushered them both out of the garage. "You guys coming?"

"No." The way Caleb gazed at me made butterflies dance in my belly. "We've got plans."

"Suit yourselves." Gabe shrugged one massive shoulder and yanked open the side door. Snow and a bitter cold wind whipped in as the door opened and shut behind them.

"Alone at last." Caleb grinned.

In a puff of black smoke he appeared in front of me and cupped my face in his hands. His lips found mine in a delicate caress. My hands wandered over his back. I reveled in the feel of his taut muscles under that thin layer of cotton.

Hot breath against my ear sent waves of euphoric bliss coursing through me as he murmured, "Are ya ready tah take a trip tah paradise, lovey?"

CHAPTER TWO

I wriggled my toes deeper into the sand and readjusted my sketchpad to get a better angle. Sea gulls screeched their high-pitched call, interrupting the sweet serenade of the gently lapping waves. A small fire crackled in front of me, more for ambiance than necessity. It was a comfortable seventy-five degrees in our tropical paradise. I glanced up from my artwork and gazed at Caleb. He strummed softly on his guitar, his skin aglow thanks to his kinship with the fire. I shook my head and cast the sketchbook aside. It was pointless. In no way could I capture his true beauty or the vitality he drew from the elements.

I leaned back on my elbows and stretched my legs out. "Are you ever going to tell me where this place actually is?"

A glossy lock of hair fell across his forehead as he looked up with the half-grin I adored. "Whar's the mystery in that, lovey? Isn't it better tah think it's just a bit o' heaven carved out for you and me?"

I closed my eyes and tipped my head back. "If it was heaven, I wouldn't have to take Dramamine to get here."

The sand crunched as Caleb set his guitar down. "The Dramamine is just so ya don't turn green when we teleport. Has nothin' to do with the end location." He rose from the rock he'd been sitting on and rounded the fire pit. His bare foot nudged my hip. "Sit up. The show's about tah start."

I pushed myself up and brushed the sand off my hands. Caleb slid behind me, and pulled me back against his chest. I took a deep breath and exhaled slowly to savor the moment. I was right where I was meant to be—where I belonged.

Purple, pink, and gold zigzags decorated the sky. Their image reflected off the water turning it the color of melted gold. "It's gorgeous."

"As are you, my love." He dotted a kiss just below my ear.

I snuggled deeper into his arms and watched as the sun disappeared behind the water's edge and the sky darkened. Unfortunately it also signaled our time together was drawing to a close. "What time is it in Tennessee?"

Caleb rocked onto his hip to slide his cell phone out of his pocket, and then clicked the screen to life. "Ya've got about thirty minutes until ya're curfew."

"Thirty minutes, huh?" In a brazen move *totally* out of character for me, I swung both my legs over one of his and tried on a saucy grin. "What could we possibly do in thirty minutes?"

"Well, not *that*." His emerald eyes burned with barely concealed desire. "'Cause this beach isn't quite *that* isolated. But there are other things … "

He freed my hair from its ponytail and weaved his fingers through it to shake the strands loose. Gently at first, his lips found mine but the heat and intensity quickly grew.

His hand slid up my leg and lingered on the curve of my hip. "Ya know," he whispered, his voice low and husky, "it's been far too long since I've made ya purr. I'm beginning to think I lost my touch."

I brushed my cheek against his and moved up to deliver a soft kiss to the tip of his ear lobe. "I'll let you in on a little secret. I've been stifling it. Didn't want you to get lazy."

His head fell back as he laughed. "Lazy? With you on me arm?" He wrapped both arms around my waist and flipped me so my back was in the sand. Raven locks fell forward and framed his handsome face when he leaned over me. "That's an impossibility if e'er there was one."

I ran my hands up his chest, over the raised ridges of the lacework of scars that decorated his torso, and linked them behind his neck. "And you love it."

In a blink his humor vanished, burned away by the intensity of his gaze. "No," he corrected. "I love *you*."

Our lips met in a fiery explosion and we lost ourselves in each other's touch. My hands raked down his back, wanting to free him from the burden of his shirt.

He caught my wandering digits and tried to pull away. "Celeste, the fire … "

"I know. It's fantastic," I murmured and reached for him again.

He swatted my hands away and nodded past me. "No, lovey, the fire. Look!"

I didn't want to look. I knew whatever it was would ruin the moment. I wasn't wrong. From within our small fire visible hands had formed. I sat up and cocked my head to watch; my eyes narrowed in confusion. The flaming fingers clawed and reached skyward, digging their way out. The fire blazed up toward the evening sky. Arms grew from the hands.

"What the heck is that?" I asked, more irritated than surprised.

"Safe to say it's demonic in nature, aye?"

"Of course it is," I grumbled.

One fire arm slammed against the sand and dragged itself in our direction. The center of the fire pit crumbled away and the head of the demon appeared—a flaming skull with vacant eye sockets and a wide grin. Horror movies had become significantly less scary since I became the Conduit.

Caleb pushed against my back. "Up we go!"

Sand kicked up as we scrambled to our feet and got some distance between the demon and us. Its fiery fingers dug into the sand to pull the lower half of its body out. Caleb shoved me behind him and held up a protective arm to keep me there—as if that would work.

Fully emerged, the demon rose up to its full height. It towered over us, a geyser of orange, yellow, and red flames that acted as a pedestal for that creepy bonehead. It raised one arm and pointed at me. Flames snapped and hissed a warning. Its sinister grin widened to something that looked like twisted delight.

"Stay behind me," Caleb ordered.

Out of the corner of my eye I noticed the diamond-shaped waves of blue that shimmered to life across the surface of Caleb's skin as he called water to him. Helpful, yes, but still not enough to make me sit out a fight.

"Yeah, right," I snorted and sidestepped him.

I didn't even have time to assume a fighting stance before a lasso of fire flew out from the demon's extended digit and cinched around my neck. The pain of my skin scorching knocked me to my knees. My fingers blistered and cracked as I scraped and clawed against the flaming noose for a whisper of air.

Through blurred, teary eyes I watched Caleb raise his palms toward me. "Just once I wish you'd listen." He unleashed a blast of water that doused me from head to toe and extinguished my assailant's weapon. Coughing and gasping for air, I tumbled forward and ate a mouthful of sand.

A puff of black smoke and Caleb was at my side. He crouched beside me, but kept his gaze fixed on the demon. "Ya a'right?"

"Do me a favor," I wheezed. "Go kill that thing."

"Gladly," my Irishman growled, then rose for battle. His shoulders squared and his chest expanded. The power of the ocean was his to beckon. The fire demon didn't stand a chance. I would've smiled if I weren't a heaping lump of prickly, writhing pain.

Mr. Flaming-Skull curled and then extended his pointer finger like he was casting out a fishing line. Flames reeled from the tip of his digit, hungrily licking their way toward Caleb. As they neared Caleb slowly raised his arms in the air. Behind the demon the formerly calm seas rose up. A lone wave materialized. It festered and churned, rushing toward the shore with the strength and speed of a freight train. The brunt of the massive tidal wave crashed down right where the demon stood. When the water rescinded, nothing remained of our blazing attacker except a lifeless skull that drifted out with the tide.

I pulled myself up to sitting. Wet sand clung to every inch of me. The pain lessened by the second, thanks to my nifty rapid healing, but it still hurt like heck. What I needed was to submerse myself in a tub filled with aloe vera.

"Just once I'd like us to have a normal date." I turned my hands over and admired the bright pink scars that now decorated them. "Free from demons, shapeshifters, muses, and anything else supernatural."

Caleb squatted down next to me and wiped sand off my cheek with his thumb. "With that criteria, lovey, neither of us would be allowed on that date."

I scowled. Yes, that was the truth. But I didn't want to hear it. Before I could open my mouth to request he leave rational thought out of this conversation thundering footfalls and snapping foliage cut me off.

"What *now*?" We both spun toward the noise on high alert.

The ground shook as a stampede of deeply tanned island folk broke through the line of palm trees. Saplings broke, palm leaves flew. Terrified men, women, and children pushed and shoved in their scrambles to get away from … something. Women desperately tried to keep hold of their screaming children in the chaos. One man fell to the ground. Some of the crowd parted, while others trampled over him.

"Well that can't be good," I grumbled under my breath and hopped to my feet.

Caleb rose beside me. His gaze fixated in the opposite direction. "I'm guessin' it has something tah do with that." He jerked his chin, motioning at the water.

I turned and followed his stare. A shape in the distance moved across the surface of the water. It had a human-like form, but couldn't be confused for a person. Partially for the whole "walking on water" thing, but mostly because of the charcoal grey storm cloud that swelled and rolled around it like a living cloak. Bursts of lightning sparked through the angry cloud. Rumbles of thunder trumpeted its arrival. The being raised one hand and drew the lightning from the cloud. Absorbing it made the shadow man spark and crackle. He raised one black, translucent arm and sent a jolt of lightning careening toward the shoreline. Sand flew as the lightning exploded not twenty feet from us.

I shook my head and *tsked*. "That's a scary lookin' dude."

"I've got this, lovey." Caleb kissed the top of my head and murmured into my wet, sandy hair. "Why don't yah make sure everyone else makes it tah safety?"

"I'll get them to safety, then I'm coming right back. You don't get to have all the fun without me," I said with a half-smile and pulled myself away to go wrangle the panicked masses.

Or … formerly panicked masses.

"Uh, Caleb?" I pointed.

He turned and gaped. "Blimey! They're like zombies!"

"Very well behaved zombies." The running and shoving stopped. The crowd slowed and walked in-land in an orderly fashion. Two gentlemen hoisted the man still sprawled on the ground to his feet. They draped his arms around their necks and ushered him along. The crowd parted and moved seamlessly around a bronze-skinned figure on the rise of a small sand dune. His hands were shoved casually in the pockets of faded jeans. The pale blue shirt he wore hung open to showcase sculpted abs.

"Miss me?" Sun-bleached hair fell across his forehead as Rowan gave me a cocky leer.

I should've known. Leave it to Rowan to turn a stampeding crowd into a bunch of trained circus monkeys without lifting a finger. An ex-member of the Dark Army, he had a talent for mind control. Fortunately, his power only worked on me when he touched me. A fact I found out the hard way. (I don't wanna talk about how.)

Rumor had it that before being turned into a half-demon member of the Dark Army he was a real life pirate. Occasionally he even broke into a bit of the lingo. Personally, I thought it was just a gimmick he used to impress girls. However, he was about as trustworthy as a pirate. Everything he did or said was in some way self-serving.

His bare feet sank into the sand as he sauntered over. Turquoise eyes gave me an appreciative once over. Caleb noticed and tensed beside me.

The intimacy of his gaze prompted me to cross my arms over my chest. "What are *you* doing here?"

"Could ask you the same thing, Poppet." One golden eyebrow rose. "Shouldn't you be drudging through snow-covered mountains, saving the world all by your lonesome?" He ran is hand through his hair, leaving it in a tangled mess of waves.

"I got the night off." Even I was surprised by my sharp and unforgiving tone. I guess Rowan brought that out in me.

Another bolt of lightning struck, this time close enough to rain sand on us. We shielded our heads until it passed.

"I'm guessin' your friend there missed that memo," Rowan said, then nodded at Caleb. The two had a very long history. For a couple hundred years, they were the closest thing to a friend each other had. "Cal, always good to see ya, mate."

"Been too long, brotha." Caleb stared out at the shadowy creature moving across the water like a tropical storm and brushed the sand from his shoulders. "Maybe we could save the reunion for af'er ya use that nifty talent of yars on that thing?"

"Wish I could." Rowan shrugged and shook grit out of his shirt.

I caught myself staring at the specks of sand that clung to his tanned and toned chest and quickly averted my gaze to the menacing shadow dude. Odd that I found *that* the safer option …

"I tried for him before I went for the crowd. Can't reach him. He must be pure demon, my ability is human specific. Without a hint of humanity in him, I can't break through." He bumped me with his shoulder. "You might want to think about that, lass. Maybe you're not as human as ya think. Could explain that touch factor."

I chose to ignore his attempt to get under my skin—right after shooting him a 'do me a favor and drop dead' glare. "So if we can't control him, what's the plan?"

Caleb's jaw flexed and his hands clenched into fists. Darkness fell over his features, giving him a dangerous and deadly appearance. "Row, get her out of here. I'll handle this."

"Uh, hello?" I snapped and shoved one hand onto my hip. "I'm the *Chosen One*, remember? Not some meek little girlie-girl that needs you to protect her."

Caleb's battle-ready exterior softened—but only for a moment. He stepped closer and pressed his palm to my cheek. "That's right. The Chosen One—whose death would both break my heart and bring about the end of the world. So, off ya go." He waved one hand to dismiss me.

If looks could kill, my boyfriend would've been on the ground twitching. *"I'm not going anywhere,"* I hissed through clenched teeth.

Caleb's eyebrows rose in expectation. He cast a sideways glance to the blond pirate. "Row?"

A hand clapped on my arm. My body fell limp and my mind went as blank as a freshly shaken *Etch-a-Sketch*. Rowan caught me and scooped me up in his arms before my head could hit the ground. Together we disappeared in a puff of black smoke.

CHAPTER THREE

As soon as my feet sank into the snow and the paralysis wore off, I spun on Rowan and slammed my fist into his stupid, chiseled jaw.

"Take me back! *Now!*"

"No can do, lass." He laughed and rubbed his reddened face. "See, most of the time I spent in that tropical haven I was slightly—correction, *majorly*—inebriated. I'm afraid I couldn't find it again if I tried."

"Oh, don't even try that!" I jabbed my finger at him, more than willing to hit him again if I thought it might help. "You know *exactly* where we were. And you're going to take me back. Because if you don't, and something bad happens to Caleb, I'm gonna snap you in two over my knee like a stick. Got it?"

Rowan leaned back and considered me through narrowed eyes. "Has anyone ever told you that you're cute when you're angry? Like a rabid teacup poodle."

I balled up my fist, ready to go all 'rabid poodle' on the other side of his smug face. Before I could arc back Grams' front door flew open. Gabe bounded out into the snow dressed only in a pair of stretchy pants. Something had him ready to morph in a moment's notice.

"There you are!" he rumbled. "Here's an idea; if you have a cell phone and happen to be the *friggin' Chosen One*, maybe you answer your phone when people call you!"

I untied my hoodie from around my waist and dug into the pocket for my phone. It frantically buzzed and shook in my palm as six missed calls, three voicemails, and over a dozen text messages came in one after the other.

"Sorry. I must've been in a dead zone. What's going on?" I tugged the hoodie up my arms, and shifted on my frozen, bare feet in the snow. "And can we maybe discuss it on the porch?" I gave Rowan a pointed stare. "I didn't get a chance to grab my shoes before getting abducted."

Instead of waiting for a response, I pushed my way between the two and trekked up to the porch. Gabe's grim tone followed me, "Cee, there've been earthquakes in New York caused by a demon. Someone caught a glimpse of it on film and all the news stations are playing it on a loop. We need to get there *now* before this turns into a world-wide panic."

I spun fast, slipped on some ice, and caught myself on the porch rail. "Three demon attacks in one night? That never happens!"

Rowan paused in buttoning his shirt to hold up one finger. "Not never. Tonight, actually."

Gabe talked right over him, not even bothering to glance his way or acknowledge his existence in the slightest. "Three? What were the other two?"

"Two demons attacked the beach Caleb and I were on. He stayed behind to deal with one and we *need* to get back and help him." I glared at Rowan who gave a noncommittal shrug.

"Cal can hold his own." Gabe's massive pecs rose and fell with each heaving breath. "We need to deal with this other matter first."

Despite it being cold enough out to see our breath, neither Gabe nor Rowan seemed chilled in the slightest. I, on the other hand, was still wet and freezing to the point of stabbing icicle pain. Pride made me try and hide it so I didn't look like the wimp. The convulsing chills probably gave my secret away.

"W-w-what I don't understand is why New York? As a r-r-rule the Dark Army attacks are centered around one of us. S-s-so why there?"

Rowan rolled his eyes and followed me up on to the porch. I flinched when he clamped his hand onto my wrist. The shaking stopped and the chills eased. Yes, my hands and feet were still blue, but I no longer *felt* the effects of the cold. I could've said thank you, but considering our history I viewed this act of kindness as the very *least* he could do.

"Maybe someone is trying to lure us there?" Gabe glared daggers at the back of Rowan's head, not happy in the least that he was touching me. "Think this is Alec or the Countess's doing?"

I chewed on my thumbnail while I mulled that over. The Countess led the Dark Army and wanted to kill me so she could basically take over the world. She could've been luring me into unfamiliar territory where I'd be vulnerable. However, Alec had been underground with his band of puppets for a while. This could've been his big reveal.

"Whoever it is wants us to know what they're up to. The demon is just a calling card. They'll make their presence known when we get there."

"Then let's go. *Now.*" Gabe's voice dripped with resentment as he finally acknowledged Rowan. "You're the fastest transportation around."

Rowan snorted a laugh and threw his hands in the air, palms up. "Sorry, mate. I've tried the hero thing before. Gave me hives. I think I'm allergic."

Gabe ground his teeth together. I guessed it was to stop his fangs from sliding down, but kept that theory to myself. "Then don't do it for you," he jerked his chin in my direction. "Do it for her."

Rowan's head fell back in a loud guffaw and he dropped my wrist. "What on earth gave you the idea *that* would work?"

My brother stomped up the porch stairs and leaned in dangerously close to the pirate. "Because you sold her out to ensure your own freedom, and she hasn't returned the favor by killing you." Gabe stood ramrod straight and stared down the bridge of his nose at Rowan. A low growl seeped out and vibrated his chest. "Unlike her, I'm not *nearly* that generous."

Despite the amused smirk Rowan wore, his eyes held a glint as deadly as a double-edged sword. "Then it's a good thing *you're* not the Conduit, aye?"

Before the oppressive testosterone in the air made me heave, I stepped between them. "Oh, for crying out loud! Would you two knock it off! Rowan, you have two choices here. You're either going to help Caleb or you're taking us to New York. It's up to you."

Rowan raised one eyebrow. "And what's to stop me from doing neither and teleporting off to some random tropical hot spot? I could have a tasty strumpet on me arm and a Mai Tai in me hand in less than ten minutes."

The front door squeaked open and Kendall poked her head out. "Uh, guys? That … thing is in Time Square and just stormed the set of *Good Morning America*. Grams called in a tizzy. Apparently if she can't start her day tomorrow with Sam Champion she's holding us, like, personally responsible. She had her scary voice on. We need to go."

"I'm working on it!" I screeched. Kendall's eyes widened and she retreated back into the house with her hands raised. I cleared my throat and tried to adopt a silky, more persuasive tone. "Rowan, Gabe's right. I do owe you a world class beat down."

"Damn right," Gabe rumbled.

I held up a finger to silence him, but kept my gaze locked on Rowan. "One you *know* I am more than capable of delivering. Someday, somewhere you and I *will* cross paths again. At that time, I'll get my payback. I promise you that. *However* … if you help me tonight I'll wipe the slate clean between us. You owe me nothing. I owe you no messy, violent death. Deal?"

"Cee, you nearly got killed because of this guy!" Gabe erupted, his face reddening in anger. "Ended up taking a fireball to the mid-section! *That ringing any bells*?!"

"Technically, that was Caleb's fault, not mine. And I also came back to save you all, let's not forget that."

"We wouldn't have needed saving if it wasn't for you!" Gabe lunged for Rowan with rage bubbling in his feline eyes like hot lava. I slammed my hands against his chest to halt him.

"Enough!" Gabe's size gave him no advantage to go around, or even through me, and we both knew it. I kept my forearm pressed to his chest and turned back to Rowan. "You have my word. You help me tonight, by first dropping us off in New York, then going back to help Caleb and we start over on neutral ground. Then, for all I care, you can poof off to find yourself that—" I felt like a dork trying on his lingo, but went for it anyway, "—*strumpet*. But if you don't do this, there will be retribution of the worst possible kind. So, what do you say? Deal?"

A wicked little spark lit Rowan's face in a way that made me wonder if I'd just made a deal with the devil as he mulled over my ultimatum. "A level playing field with the Conduit herself?" His mouth curled into a wry smile. "Hmmmm ... that's too tempting to pass up. Not having to watch over my shoulder for when you're finally going to pounce ... "

"Don't flatter yourself. I wouldn't pounce. I'd drop kick you."

He licked his lips as if the very idea sounded scrumptious. "Either way, pack a lunch kiddies, we're heading to the Big Apple."

CHAPTER FOUR

"It's everything I dreamed of!" Kendall spun in a circle, her arms thrown out wide. "The hustle and bustle of the big city! The high-rises! The fashion! Broadway!" She pulled her arms in and hugged herself. "Oh, Broadway. That was my dream before I grew wings. Hey! That could be a great idea for a play!"

"Kendall, we're in a dark, dingy alley that smells like gym socks and pickles." I kept my hands stuffed into my pockets out of fear of catching some rare skin-eating virus. "You haven't actually seen New York yet."

"Still." She shrugged with stars in her eyes. "We're here. I can *feel* it."

Gabe grimaced like Kendall smelled worse than the alley. "Let's go over the plan again, so we can get out of here ASAP."

"I'm finding this field trip very enlightening." Rowan rocked back on his heels and stuffed his hands into the pockets of the winter jacket he'd borrowed from Gabe. The three-sizes-too-big coat dwarfed him to the point that his demonhood seemed a bit diminished. "The whole demonic community would be significantly less intimidated by your little group if they spent an evening with you."

Gabe's head whipped around and a menacing growl tore its way out of his solid wall of a chest. In a blink his eyes turned to topaz. Rowan said nothing, but cocked his head and raised one eyebrow, daring my brother to advance.

25

Caleb still being in jeopardy shortened my patience with their testosterone charged crap down to exactly zero. "I get it! We *all* get it. That garbage can over there gets it! You don't like each other. Well, big friggin' deal! We've got a job to do! So, as of right now you're gonna stop with the snide comments, *and* the growling, or you're both gonna find out what a groin kick delivered by the Chosen One feels like. Got it?"

Silence. Then Gabe cleared his throat and physically shook off his feline attributes.

Rowan swung his arms around and ended with a casual *snap/clap*. "To answer your earlier question, I believe the brilliant plan our fearless leader came up with was to grab the disgusting, evil creature and give him the equivalent of a group hug so I can whisk us all away to a more private location where we can kill him in a horribly bloody manner, yes?"

A deep scowl creased my forehead. "Well, when you say it like that it sounds stupid."

Rowan made no attempts to disguise how funny he found this. "Doesn't matter how I say it, doll. You plan to snuggle the enemy. Clearly, this idea is flawed."

"News crews and cops are swarming Time Square trying to get a good view of this thing." I didn't actually need to defend myself to him—or anyone really—but I hated having my battle plans called into question. It made me justifiably argumentative and downright cranky. Then again, that might just be the effects a' la Rowan. "Up to this point it has moved fast enough to appear as nothing more than a humongous, blurred thing to them *and* their cameras. But we can't fight in front of a crowd like that and maintain any kind of anonymity."

Rowan took a step forward, right smack dab into my comfort zone. His leer, meant solely to entice, for some reason brought to mind the serpent tempting Eve to take a bite of the apple. "So, let 'em all see what you can do. Let 'em marvel at the wonder that is the Conduit." His gaze dragged leisurely over me. His turquoise eyes glittered with naughty suggestions. I stayed put and tried to act completely indifferent to his brazenness rather than risk riling Gabe up again. "They'd adore you, lass. And flock to worship at your alter. You could live as a goddess among men. Why not?"

I smiled in spite of myself when I realized that idea held no appeal to me. My calling gave me a peace and clarity of my path that few people ever found. "Because I have a higher calling and it's a heck of a lot more important than me ending up on *E! News Daily.*"

Kendall sucked in a shocked breath. How dare I speak ill of her beloved *E!*.

I rolled my eyes, but stayed on with my original point. "To protect our identities and to keep all these people safe we're going to take that thing far away from here to kill it."

Rowan's expression contorted in a swirling mess of confusion and disgust. "And there's nothing in it for you?"

"Not really. No."

"Yet you do it voluntarily?" With the judgmental, condescending tone he used, you would have thought I just admitted to gargling with razor blades.

I pressed my lips together and nodded.

"Whatever blows your skirt up, Poppet." He shrugged. "As for me, I need to get this little hero mission over with and go find myself some fun form of debauchery to revel in. I hang around you all too long and I may catch morals." He faked a shiver. Then, with a smile that bordered on villainous, he added, "Now let's go snuggle your big, nasty beastie."

∛ ✳ √

"*Liberty Island?!* You got us as far as Liberty Island?" A hooked claw swished over my head. I ducked before it could skewer my brain.

"There's no one here and I couldn't hold him any longer!" Rowan hollered from under the shield of his arms. "Even in smoke form he managed to bite me. *What is that thing?*"

With his lip curled to reveal razor sharp teeth, Gabe-lion galloped toward the beast. The creature swung its horns and hooked Gabe under his front legs. It stomped through the snow, then flung him at the water's edge. Gabe dug his claws into the frozen ground as he skidded. Inches were all that prevented him from plunging into the icy Upper Bay.

"My best guess is that at some point a bat and a water buffalo got together and had a love child that could miraculously walk on two legs." With one arm still defensively raised, I pointed with the opposite hand. "That would be their love spawn."

"Well, whatever it is, it's cranky we interrupted its tirade and brought it here." Rowan scooted around to position me between the Bat-bull and himself. Nobility was obviously not a personality trait he bothered with. "Did I mention what a monumentally bad idea this was?"

"It came up!" I shrieked as the Bat-bull pivoted around and thundered at us on heavy hooved feet. "Kendall! Little help here!"

Kendall sat huddled in her winged cocoon by Lady Liberty's big toe. Feathers parted and one blue eye peeked out. "You can come in here. I'll scoot, but I'm not coming out!"

"Oh, that's nice. *Shield!*" I hollered and leapt in the air. Pulling into a tight tuck I spun over the head of the incoming Bat-bull. Rowan disappeared in a puff of smoke a second before the beast plowed into him.

Our lion—slightly disheveled from his fall—trotted up at the same moment Rowan reappeared behind me. "Now that you got him here, oh-wise Conduit, what are you going to do with him?"

Snow kicked up when the Bat-bull screeched to a halt and spun back in our direction. A white cloud of hot air puffed from his wide, smooshed nose. Red eyes glared from big bovine sockets. He tossed his head to intimidate us with the massiveness

28

of glossy black horns. I couldn't speak for the others, but that intimidation tactic worked wonders on me. Every time it charged I forgot how to use my abilities and my feeble mind only manage one thought—*run!*

"I suggest we figure out how to kill him before he kills us!" I squealed in an octave only dogs could hear.

One back hoof pawed at the ground, yet this time the beast didn't charge. Instead it raised its two-fingered hands high in the air. Coal-black flesh gave way to ridged and curved talons. In one swift motion it arched back then slammed its hands to the ground. Those claws sliced through the frozen earth like it was softened butter.

Beside me Gabe tensed and sniffed deeply at the air. Whatever his Spidey Sense detected caused his muzzle to curl up in a threatening growl.

Before I could form the words, "Golly, Gabe, what's the matter?" the ground began to shake. Our lion locked his legs to steady himself. Both Rowan and I fell to our knees. Bone-chillingly cold water sloshed up in protest of the quaking ground. It rained down on us in a shower that cut like knives. I glanced over at Lady Liberty, deeply hoping she was sturdy enough to withstand the tremors. So far the big broad was held up, but I needed to make this stop before she reached her limit.

On my hands and knees, I crawled to Rowan and latched onto his wrist. "Drop me off right in front of it."

Golden hair bounced over his forehead and into his eyes. "I can't tell if you're insanely brave or suicidal."

I peered back at the Bat-bull and pondered the same thing. "Right now, let's go with brave. But make it quick before I change my mind and make Keni fly me out of here."

"Keni would be totally okay with that!" her muffled voice interjected from behind down covered "walls".

Rowan hooked an arm around my waist and poofed us to the foot of the beast. I *thought* I'd have a few seconds to initiate an offensive attack. I did not. Turns out the Bat-bull had surprisingly quick reflexes for such a big fella. Before I could get my bearings, it retracted its claws and attacked. My hands caught its horns a second before it gored me. Momentum knocked me to the ground, and I took the Bat-bull with me. I held firm as the beast tossed and turned to free its head. Up close its squished bat-face was even more grotesque. Plus, this dude smelled foul. Like soured milk left in the sun to bake. Judging by the eardrum splitting squeak it was making, I guessed it was enjoying our close encounter about as much as I was. If my hands weren't busy pushing its chin to its chest so it couldn't see to shred me with its wildly flailing claws I would've covered my ears. Battle can be downright inconvenient at times.

Gabe danced around the perimeter of the battle, anxiously anticipating his opportunity to jump in; preferably one that wouldn't lead to him accidentally chomping his sister. Rowan, on the other hand, stood so close he could've poked the Bat-bull with his borrowed boot. Yet there he stood, texting away with a rather bored, disconnected look on his face.

"Little help here?" I grunted.

The pirate sucked air through his teeth. "Sorry, doll. I'm like your demonic cab driver. Here to give ya a lift, but not getting involved in your goings on. By the way, the meter is *definitely* running. Aren't I supposed to scurry off to save your beau?"

"This is why people don't like you." A goober of foamy Bat-bull spittle dripped down onto my jacket, prompting an immediate dry-heave.

I needed out from under this guy *now*, if not sooner. Wriggling and straining, I maneuvered my knees up to my chest.

"We will save Caleb—*oof*—together." I managed to get my feet positioned just right and used a little extra oomph to kick the monstrous dude off of me, "Right after I kill this thing."

One of its horns snapped off in my hand and the creature went airborne … for a second. It landed on its feet. Red eyes burned with rage as it pawed at the earth and snorted in my general direction.

30

I sprang off the ground and landed in a defensive stance, the horn grasped firmly in my hand. The creature flipped his head and charged. Padded feet thumped up beside me and a slow smile of renewed confidence spread across my face. My feline sentry finally found his in.

"I'll go high, you go low!" Together we sprinted at the incoming beast.

We had fought side by side enough to know each other's battle strategies. Not a sound or syllable had to be uttered. Instinct led us to jump at exactly the same moment. I put my shoulder in and hit the Bat-bull square in the chest. Gabe took out its legs.

The creature hit the ground with a loud, "*Huuuunnnhhh!*"

Our combined force was enough to bring it down, but barely enough to keep it there. The thrashing creature bucked violently beneath us. In a move that would've gotten us kicked out of any superhero league—if there was such a thing—we sprawled on top of it. A suave and cool move? No. But effective.

Knowing it was more Gabe's weight than mine keeping the beast down, I turned my body and wedged the flat side of its broken horn against its windpipe. Its thrashing grew spastic and reckless. It didn't take long for lack of oxygen to win out. Glowing red eyes dimmed and rolled back into its bovine head.

"I'd stop short of killing him if I were you," a silky, sultry voice suggested.

Rowan snapped up, ramrod straight. His hands balled into fists and his arms pulled away from his body, ready to strike. "*Countess.*"

Despite the awkward angle, I craned my head around. There she stood. The evil villainess that turned an entire army of mortals into her own band of demonic minions programmed to create carnage and destruction as she saw fit. She possessed an incomprehensible amount of power, yet chose to dress like a skank. Skintight black leather pants disappeared into matching thigh-high boots. A satin ivory corset drew her tiny waist in and

31

hugged her hourglass shape. Her leather fetish continued with a plum jacket that covered her arms, but stopped just below her full breasts. Many cows died so she could look like a high- priced call girl from Hell.

Her complexion held the same flawless luminescence of polished marble. Thick crimson hair waved down her back like a velvet curtain. The glowing red of her eyes made her a kind of beautiful that could only be described as demented.

"Rowan," she cooed and licked her wine-painted lips. "Always a pleasure."

His body jerked in response, as if hearing his name spew from her lips caused a physical reaction.

The Countess ignored his discomfort and swung her gaze my way. "*Bestiarequiesce!*"

Beneath me the Bat-bull went limp. All the fight left his body... and he seemed to be snoring.

She gave me a smile reminiscent of a snake eyeing a field mouse. "You can let him go. He's no longer a threat to you."

I peered down at the drooling Bat-bull, then pulled the horn away from his throat and rose to my feet. Fur brushed the back of my hand as Gabe took his place beside me.

"I take it he's your toy." I jerked my chin at the sleeping demon. Its hands and feet kicked at the air as if it was dreaming about chasing a rabbit.

"He is," she confirmed, her hands resting on her ample hips. "But not just *any* toy. One of great value. To me..." she savored the remaining words before she revealed them, "...*and* to you."

The flap of feathers, a gust of wind, and Keni landed beside me. A big enough danger was all it took for my Protector to grow a spine and return. "We don't value demons. At least not ones that look and smell like that ...'cause *ick*."

"That's only because you haven't been properly introduced to him." The Countess paced in front of us, her stiletto boots crunching across the snow covered ground. "This is Cronus.

Celeste has had the pleasure of meeting a couple of his brothers tonight. Namely Lapetes and the dearly departed Menoetius." She turned my way and stared straight into my eyes, "They happen to be...Titans."

My chest tightened. The drumming thud of my heart pounded in my ears. It took everything I had to keep my face at neutral. "Caleb."

"Correct!" Eerily white teeth flashed with her smile. "The *exact* kind of demon your hunky boyfriend has in him. Isn't that a fun coincidence!" Her nose crinkled like we were two girlfriends gossiping.

Keni's blonde head lobbed back and forth from the Countess, to me, and back again. "Wait ... what does that mean?"

"It means that one of them is linked to Caleb. Its blood is in his veins. If the demon he's linked to dies, it's buh-bye to your fine Irish lad." The Countess pressed one deadly sharp fingernail to her lip and pretended to mull it over. "You know, for the life of me I can't remember which one it was. We branded *a lot* of young boys with demon blood that day." She threw her hands in the air and chuckled. "After all this time, how could I be expected to keep them all straight? Anyhow, it'd be a real pity for you to kill the wrong one. You got lucky when you slaughtered Menoetius. But next time a Titan dies Caleb might just tag along with them."

At that very moment Caleb was on the beach fighting with the Shadow dude ... another Titan. If he killed it ... *No.* I couldn't even think it. Urgency left no time for words. Empathically I slapped Rowan with a deep-seeded need to get Caleb *now*. Concern shadowed his face and he disappeared in a puff of smoke as the message penetrated his thoughts.

"I do hope he hurries," she purred with an over dramatic sigh. "It'd be such a waste of a fine specimen of manhood. But really, girl, did you think I was just going to let him walk away from my army? From *me*?"

Unable to contain it a moment longer, my anger boiled to the surface and erupted. "*Why?!* Why are you doing this? How is hurting him going to help you harness the Gryphon's powers? This is between you, me, and the Gryphon. Let Caleb *go*!"

Her smile faltered. She drew her crimson eyebrows drew together and cocked her head to the side. "You still don't know what this is really about, do you?"

The snarky words left my lips before my brain could filter them. "Other than you being a power hungry witch that dresses like she went to an S&M yard sale? Nope, that's all I've got."

In a flash she was in my face, close enough for me to see green flames flickering in her blood red irises. "You smart mouthed little twit. You shouldn't speak of things you don't understand. Did you ever ask the Council the truth about your precious Gryphon and the things he has done? *Have you*?!"

I raised my chin and tried my best to look unaffected. I didn't want to be frightened by her. It was my calling *not* to be. But my knees were knocking so loud I suspected she could hear them.

She took a deep breath, closed her eyes and let it out slowly. Then, with her composure once again intact, she began, "My motivation runs deeper than simply coveting his abilities. I have all the power I could ever need. I gathered it with one goal in mind ... *revenge*. Revenge against the very beast you have sworn to protect." For a split second a hint of sadness seemed to crack her stone exterior. "Perhaps when your Celtic cutie dies you'll see how motivating a forced revenge can be."

Crimson hair curtained her face as she bowed her head to Cronus. I couldn't help but wonder if that move was intentional to hide her seeping humanity. "*Orior oriri ortus meus pet.*"

The bat-bull's eyes snapped open and a visible puff of air expelled from his broad nostrils.

Façade firmly back in place, the Countess tossed her hair and stared down at me with her regal Queen of the Damned posture restored. "For the sake of your raven-haired love I hope you can refrain from killing Cronus. However, rest assured that more Titans *will* follow and you can't save them all. Sooner or later, Caleb *will* die. Do yourself a favor and come to terms with that, girl. "

After a quick little finger wave she vanished into the night and her heaving beast rose up to attack.

CHAPTER FIVE

Gabe-lion stalked up beside me and plopped down with a huff. His massive head turned my way, and he heaved an exasperated breath directly at me.

"Yeah, I know." I rubbed my frozen arms and scooted closer to my big, hairy brother. "I probably should've reminded Rowan to come back for us."

"Ya think?" Kendall's teeth chattered through blue lips. Her ivory wings encompassed her like a shawl, but couldn't hinder the biting cold.

"You could always try to fly us out of here instead of just sitting there like a lump," I snapped, my tone sharpened by my deep desire to regain feeling in my toes.

"I can't lift Gabe," she grumbled, turning her back to me to end the conversation.

If my face wasn't frozen like Jack Nicholson's at the end of *The Shining* I might have smiled. Despite her griping, Kendall would sit right here and freeze alongside us until help came. She could fly off at any moment, but her soft heart wouldn't let her. However, if Rowan didn't get his butt back here soon I planned to use my empathic ability to overthrow her sweetness and motivate her to fly off and commandeer a ferry to come pick us up.

I was eyeing the shoreline for a vessel to target for that very reason, when a puff of black smoke materialized at the base of Lady Liberty. I leapt up onto frozen feet that screamed in painful protest when I put weight on them.

Rowan unceremoniously deposited three of Grams' heaviest afghans onto the snow covered ground. "Those are for you." He rubbed his hands together and warmed them with his breath. "Tad nippy out here, isn't it?"

"Really? We hadn't noticed." I scooped up the blankets and shook off the snow. One went to Gabe, who morphed underneath it and wrapped it around himself, one to Keni who flung hers over her wings for an extra layer of warmth, and I wrapped mine around my shoulders.

"Where's Caleb?" My voice quaked and this time it couldn't be blamed on the cold.

"Romeo is at your Grannie's house recovering. A lesser man would've perished after taking a dozen or so lightning bolt hits, but not our Cal. He gave as good as he got and remained esthetically pleasing all the while ... for the most part." Waves of golden hair poked out from under a grey and blue knit beanie cap I recognized as one of the extras Grams knitted while she watched her stories.

A grunt and wheeze behind us made Rowan's head swivel around. "*What in blazes did you do to him?*"

Cronus—who will always be Bat-bull to me—was sprawled on the ground, covered in feathers. He lifted his head, arms, and legs maybe an inch off the ground as he snorted, grunted, and strained, but couldn't budge beyond that.

"It would seem Keni's feathers are like a force field to him."

"Celeste ripped a bunch out by the handful!" Keni pouted and rubbed the bald spot on the tip of her right wing.

"Oh, they'll grow back, ya big baby. It was that or let him gore us to death. I think it was pretty fast thinking!"

"And *I* think I'm gonna shave your head in your sleep and see how *you* like being bald."

"Yeah, cause that's the same!"

"Ladies!" Gabe yelled, chills racking his mammoth frame. "Can we *please* have this conversation at home? When I have pants on?"

Rowan held up one hand to shield his eyes. "Lots of holes in that blanket, mate. Just so ya know."

Gabe's complexion went from blue to purple and he readjusted his blankie.

"We should scurry along though. Your soon-to-be bride and that angry little wee man are both in quite a tizzy."

All I wanted to do was get home and see Caleb alive and in one piece. But my sacred duty made it mandatory for me to ask, "About what?"

Rowan stared at me like I just had a sudden flare up of stupid. "I didn't ask. That would imply caring, which we've established I do *not*."

I smacked my forehead with the palm of my hand. "That's right. How could I forget for even a split second what a major tool you are? Well come on Cap'n Sensitivity, let's get us home so you can go back to spreading your charm the world over."

"So we're not gonna be BFFs after this?" Rowan said with a mock pout. "I was so looking forward to the slumber parties and pillow fights."

"Me too." I tightened my afghan around my shoulders as we three Garrett kids circled our proverbial supernatural taxicab. "Spoiler alert; there was a brick in mine."

"What about him?" Gabe jerked a thumb at Cronus.

I stared over my shoulder at the flutter-kicking monster. "We'll tell Bernard about him. If the Countess doesn't come and claim him maybe the Council will have an idea of what to do. Otherwise we come back tomorrow and have Keni hug him into submission so we can move him."

A second before we dissipated in a cloud of smoke Keni raised her hand in the air. "I vote we leave him here and make him a New York tourist attraction."

CHAPTER SIX

Bernard, Alaina, and Grams—who came home from her boyfriend's in light of the chaos—all tried to intercept me when I walked in the door. Each chattered away at top speed.

I didn't even pretend to listen, just silenced them with a raised hand and stern look. "Where is he?"

Grams pressed her pink painted lips together and pointed toward her bedroom. I pushed past them and bee-lined it down the hall. If they voiced a complaint I didn't bother to listen—or care.

My hand closed around the doorknob. I took a deep breath to prepare myself for the worst and then pushed it open. One glance was all it took to steal a shocked gasp from my parted lips. He lay on the bed uncovered and still as a corpse. Gram's white orchard print comforter was folded at his feet, probably because even the light touch of it would've been rough against his vast burns and abrasions. His chest rose and fell with a movement so faint I had to step closer and stare hard to confirm he *was* breathing. Grey shadows circled his sunken eyes. All color had been sucked from his complexion leaving him a chalky white.

Tentatively I approached the bed, afraid that even the air I expelled would cause him further pain. Grams had cleaned and dressed his wounds. A small bandage protected a wound on his left cheek, just under his eye. His left arm required a larger dressing held by a plethora of hospital tape. Black scorch marks streaked out from under his wrapped right shoulder. White cotton gauze covered his entire abdomen. It had to be a nasty wound to warrant a bandage that size. I gently brushed the hair from his forehead. As much as I hated to see him like this, the events of the night could've ended *much* worse.

His heavy lidded eyes fluttered open in response to my touch. "Lovey," he croaked in a weak, raspy whisper. "I'm tryin' out a new charbroiled look. What do ya think?"

I shook my head. Tears blurred my vision, but I blinked them back before they fell. "I'm not a fan. Do you … " I choked on the words and swallowed hard to free them. "Does it hurt?"

His ebony brows drew together. A deep crease formed between his eyes. "It did. But then ya'r grandmum gave me a handful of assorted pills. Now I can't feel me head, or anythin' else for that matter."

I erupted in a way too loud guffaw. "Your head's still there. I promise."

He raised one hand off the bed and turned it palm up. I laid my own in it and forced a smile despite the heaviness weighing on my heart. "Thank ya for sendin' Rowan back. If he wouldn't have gotten there when he did I might not have made it out alive. He told me if I had killed that thing I *still* could've died. That's a no-win situation if e'er there was one."

What he meant as a light-hearted joke caused a knot of pain to swell in my stomach. I had—and would continue to—endured great trials and agonies because of my calling. But I couldn't lose Caleb. He was my anchor in a sea of chaos.

I fought to keep my voice steady in an effort not to upset him in his battered state. "Rowan said you and the Titan exchanged lightning bolts. I didn't know you could do that."

The corners of Caleb's pale lips tugged back in a weak grin. "Guess we hadn't reached the 'I can shoot lightnin' out of my finger tips' portion of our relationship yet."

"Guess not." I dragged the tip of my index finger across his hand, tracing the blue veins visible through his skin.

Without warning his eyes widened in panic and his features darkened. "Celeste, that thing is still at the beach! We have tah go back tah that village! It could be terrorizin' those people." He started to rise up off the bed, but I caught his shoulders and eased him back down. It took surprisingly little effort which made my heart ache at his weakened state. "We have tah stop it!"

"We will, we will," I soothed. "Just as soon as we figure out how to do that without killing you in the process, okay? We'll figure something out. I promise."

He stopped fighting and settled back onto the pillow. Either his pain meds kicked in or that little display zapped the last of his energy. Whatever the cause, his blinks became excessively long and his voice grew heavy with sleep. "Ya promise?"

I ran my fingers through his silky locks and gave him a reassuring smile that I knew didn't reach my eyes. "I'll go talk to Bernard right now. We'll figure this out. You just rest."

"Just a quick rest. Wake me as soon as you hear somethin'." His eyes shut and I doubted they'd open back up any time soon.

I leaned in to dot a quick kiss on his forehead and inhaled his pungent scent of charcoal and *Neosporin*. I let my gaze wander over the planes of his face and said a silent prayer of thanks that the arrogant, untrustworthy, self-centered, too-pretty-for-his-own-good pirate got to Caleb on time. Battered I could handle, dead I could not. In that moment I vowed to myself that I would find a way to save him.

CS ✳ SO

No one in the living room spoke or made eye contact. The only sound came from the television murmuring quietly in the background. Gabe had dressed in jeans and a sweatshirt. Alaina sat huddled on his lap, her eyes red-rimmed from crying. He held her tight, offering the only comfort he could while the life of her *only* sibling hung in the balance.

Grams sat in her leather recliner, her freshly painted nails rested in her lap. The grim set of her mouth did nothing to reassure me. Shockingly, Rowan was still there. He leaned against the doorway that led to the foyer, as if prepared to bolt at a moment's notice. Apparently the brotherhood he forged with Caleb over the years ran deeper than his selfish desires—for now. In the center of the room Bernard paced back and forth on Grams' thick nap white rug. His tiny cane sank in a good inch with each purposeful step. Kendall, dressed in her two-piece pink flamingo pajamas with slits cut for her wings, lounged on the floor beside the couch. Her wings hung limp behind her as she massaged the spot where I ripped her feathers out. The area was still red, but soft fuzzy down had begun to grow back.

She glanced up. Her blue eyes deep pools of sadness and sorrow. "I'm sorry I can't heal him for you."

I plopped down on the floor beside her, reached over and pulled her wing toward me. I traumatized the darn thing, the least I could do was take a turn massaging it. "He's a demon. Your powers won't work on him." I nudged her with my shoulder. "I know you'd heal him if you could."

She nodded through her tears.

A red-faced Bernard spun on me. His words spewed from his mouth as if he couldn't hold them back a second longer. "Conduit, this matter is of dire importance! Demons are walking among civilians, causing mayhem and destruction, yet you sit here doing nothing because of *him*!" He jabbed a short, stubby finger towards Grams' bedroom.

I bit my tongue hard enough to taste blood, but fought to keep my composure—aka not punt the gnome. Instead I purposely focused my gaze on Kendall's injured wing. "I know where you're going with this, Bernard, and I suggest you take that idea and shove it … "

"There's a way to save him!"

My head snapped up so fast I'm surprised I didn't give myself whiplash. "Okay...didn't see you going there."

Determination burned in his beady eyes. "We need you out there fighting and ridding the world of the Titans and you will only do that if that boy can remain safe. Is this correct?"

Shocked and downright confused, I forced myself to muster a slight nod.

"If he's open to the sacrifice it will require, he can be saved."

Despite her lack of feathers, Alaina flew off Gabe's lap with a bird-like elegance. Her long auburn ponytail swayed from the rapid movement. She twisted the hem of Gabe's Detroit Lions football jersey with anxious hands. "A binding incantation? If he agrees it would free him from the Titans forever!"

Alaina's exuberant reaction made me feel this was a matter I should be standing for. I dropped Kendall's wing and rose to my feet. "*What?* How?"

"He has to agree to bind the demon within him and let it be destroyed." Alaina's mouth opened to add something, but she quickly clamped it shut.

"That's a good thing, right? He'd be free and I could kick some Titan butt all the way back to the Underworld."

Alaina's shoulders slumped, her fidgeting hands stilled. Bernard cleared his throat and stared at the TV, suddenly very interested in what was happening on *Jersey Shore*. Gabe, Kendall, Grams, and I exchanged confused looks at the piece of this puzzle we were obviously missing.

Rowan pushed himself off the wall with an exasperated sigh. "What they don't want to tell ya, Poppet, is that he'll then be *human* and as vulnerable as a newborn babe."

Ice ran through my veins. I shook my head slowly at first, but it quickly progressed into me spastically flicking my head from side to side. "No. Absolutely not. Not an option. Not after what happened to Alec. I worry constantly about Grams and Alaina being in the middle of all this demonic crap. But Caleb was one of them! He's viewed as a traitor. Being human would be a death sentence. We have to find another way."

Alaina slammed her balled up fist against her leg. "There *is* no other way! The Titans are going to keep coming. You *have* to stop them, and if you don't let us bind Caleb's demon first he'll die!"

"I'm not going to help you paint a bull's-eye on Cal's back," Rowan spat through his teeth, then vanished in a puff of smoke.

Bernard stood on his tiptoes to place a calming hand on Alaina's arm and spoke in a reluctant whisper. "There is something we could do. It will be exceedingly difficult for you all, but it *will* keep Caleb safe from harm."

She clasped his tiny hand, her voice bubbling with hopeful expectation. "Anything! I'll do anything! Just name it."

Bernard slowly pulled his hand away and folded both in front of him. He pressed his joined hands to his lips and peered at me with a weary gaze. "Celeste..." This must be serious, he had never called me by my name before. Honestly, I didn't think he even knew it. "You know the Gryphon has the ability to cloak reality. That's how he hides the entrance to the Spirit Plane. After we destroy the demon within Caleb—if you are willing—the Gryphon could create an entirely new identity for him. Far from the dark forces that could harm him. Unfortunately that will also take him away from ... you."

My heart momentarily forgot how to beat and my breath caught. To protect him I had to lose him? I went on autopilot and struggled to manage coherent thought in light of this new revelation. "How can we be assured the army won't find him?"

Bernard leaned on his cane with compassion and understanding in his eyes that I didn't know him capable of. "His energy and every aspect of him will be cloaked. Even if the Countess herself walked up to him she would get no traces or inklings of his true identity."

"And if *I* saw him?" My voice betrayed me by cracking.

"You wouldn't recognize him, and he won't remember you," Bernard cocked his head and attempted to reassure me, "but he'll be safe."

Alaina grasped my arm hard enough to leave white indentations. "We *have* to do it, Celeste! We have to protect him!"

Her willingness to accept this so easily while a knife of pain hacked away at my heart only angered me. "Even though it means losing him forever? You're okay with that? What if it was Gabe? Would you let him go?"

She dropped her hand and glanced over her shoulder at my brother. "If his life was at risk I'd do whatever it took to keep him safe. No matter what."

The couple exchanged loving gazes that only added fuel to the fire of my irritation. "Well I guess you're better people than me for being so willing to sacrifice your relationship."

Grams rose from her chair and flung her arm around my shoulders to squeeze me tight. Normally her nearness calmed me, made me feel protected and loved. Right now it only added more stimuli in a stressful situation that had me teetering dangerously close to my breaking point. "We all care about Caleb and want to keep him safe, honey. You just have to give it some thought and decide what's best for *him*."

"No," a weak voice interrupted.

We all turned. Caleb stood in the hallway, the palm of his hand pressed against the wall to steady himself.

While I had done nothing wrong, I still shifted guiltily under the weight of his stare. "No one is decidin' what's best for me except me."

"But, Cal ... " Alaina tried to interrupt, but was silenced by his glare.

"I'll happily become human and give up the burden of my demon half. But I won't leave Celeste. If I have tah die tah keep her safe, that's exactly what I'll do. But until then I'm not goin' anywhere."

"Then you won't become human." I shrugged out of Grams embrace and crossed my arms over my chest.

We locked eyes. The bullheaded Irishman stared with an infuriating stern scowl. His adamant stance on this issue didn't faze me. I'd sooner walk through fire than allow Caleb to become human.

CHAPTER SEVEN

"You can, and should, make this decision for him. But you won't because of your feelings for him."

"We are not having this conversation again. Besides, this isn't even you talking. It's Alaina. When did you become her overly hairy messenger?"

"I'm not her messenger. We're a couple, and couples should communicate and make their decisions as a team."

"I see she's still making you watch *The View*."

"Shut up. Some of those women make very good points."

"Sure they do. Now please keep your voice down. You're going to blow our cover." I shifted on the balls of my feet and peeked out the window of the lifeguard shack. Sand blew and churned outside with enough force to leave welts on skin. What civilians thought was nothing more than a nasty storm ravaged the Florida Gulf Coast line. Waves slammed against the shore, each swell larger than the last. But this was no normal tropical storm. Another Titan could be thanked for this onslaught, one that held power over the water.

These situations had been commonplace ever since that night at Grams when Caleb and I had a *massive* fight over his humanity. Much screaming occurred and no resolution whatsoever was reached. It ended when he claimed I was a, "Stubborn woman that let her emotions override common sense."

I came back with the rebuttal of, "Yeah? So's your face."

Unable to form any kind of rebuttal to that, Caleb threw his hands in the air and stomped off.

Over the next two weeks Gabe, Keni, and I traveled to various spots around the globe to deal with natural disasters caused by Titans. Caleb joined us as soon as he healed enough to fight. Together we stopped a tsunami in Thailand, an earthquake in Oklahoma, a tornado in Texas, and a wildfire in California. Our latest stop thwarting mission led us to a hurricane in the Sunshine state. It worked in our favor that the local media blamed these freak weather related bouts on climate issues caused by global warming. We saved the world and inadvertently raised awareness. Go us!

Rarely were we allowed the luxury of rest. No sooner would we get one matter under control than another would pop up. I missed sleep, a wonderfully delightful task I sincerely hoped to get reacquainted with soon.

"Blow our cover?" Gabe snorted and yanked off his t-shirt to prepare for his change. "We're hiding. The Chosen One is hunkered down out of sight like a scared little kid. We should be killing these things. Not subduing them until Bernard comes along and blinks them off to God only knows where."

I ducked back down and leaned my forehead against the window ledge. A few deep breaths helped me regain control of my rapidly rising blood pressure. To keep Caleb safe we went for the knockout instead of the kill. I hated holding back during battles, but if it kept Caleb alive it was worth it. Bernard agreed to help us by transporting the demons to a plane where they couldn't harm anyone. Yet everyday a new wave of them came at us with no signs of the onslaught slowing or stopping.

I glanced over my shoulder at Gabe and gave him an easy to read 'drop it' look. "I'm respecting Caleb's wishes. You should tell *his sister* to give it a try."

"Actually, his wish was to be human, but you gave him the death stare and clucked at him like a demented hen for even suggesting that."

"Human isn't an option, not with the chaos going on right now. And we're done talking about this." I glared at my brother and hoped that would be the moment the Gryphon bestowed death-ray laser vision on me.

He held his hands up in surrender. "Hey, I'm just stating the facts. No need to call forth the PMS Queen."

A fireball blazed into the sky from a shack further down the beach. It saved Gabe from getting a punch to the throat for that remark. "There's the signal. Time to go."

Instantly we became all business. The savage roar of the wind muted the sickening snaps and pops of Gabe's transformation. I shuffled on my hands and knees to the door. It took both hands and a fair amount of super strength to pry it open. What I saw on the other side made my jaw swing open and my bladder control threaten to fail.

"*Celeste, look out!*" someone—I'm fairly certain me—screamed.

I shook my head in an attempt to erase the unbelievable image before me. A shark surfed toward me on top of a wave. Sharks can't surf, I know that. But—terrifying as it was—this one excelled at it. The wide open mouth of a Great White, if I had to guess, soared my way ready to devour me. My legs forgot how to move and my brain switched into an operating speed the equivalent of a hamster running on an exercise wheel. Fear paralyzed me where I stood.

The black eyes of the gigantic fish rolled back in their sockets as its rows of razor sharp teeth extended out, hungry for my flesh. A mighty roar pierced the air as my lion sentry soared over my head and intercepted the killer fish. He hit it head on and the two rolled across the sand in a frenzied explosion of gnashing teeth and snapping jaws. Only then did I realize the shark sported legs.

So that's what a Water Titan looks like—pants wetting terrifying.

The two savage beasts clung together. Both sets of bone-crushing teeth snarled and grappled to tear into the other's flesh.

Wet sand clung to them as they blurred together in their violent flurry. A flash of a silver fin. The swipe of a tawny claw. The flip of a long tail fin. Flying chunks of chestnut fur.

Caleb and Kendall ran across the beach. Keni's wings shielded them from the hammering winds and sea spray. They didn't need to hurry. None of us could do anything. Getting between the shark and lion would mean a loss of limbs ... or a nasty flare up of deadness. I tried to part them with my telepathy, but even mental means couldn't get between them. I could do nothing but watch—until the unthinkable happened.

The shark flung its head to the side and sunk its teeth deep into Gabe's hip. Our lion roared in pain. Blood bubbled and poured from his gaping wound. Muscle and tissue ripped from bone and hung off him like limp spaghetti noodles. Bile rose in my throat and I slapped my hand over my mouth. Instinct prompted my feet into action. I rushed to my brother's aid but quickly found he had no need for me. His lip curled up and he lunged on the shark. The pupils of his feline eyes dilated and blood lust took over. Claws and teeth shredded and devoured the fish's course skin in a violent fury. Blood sprayed through the air and splattered me from head to toe.

"Gabe! *Stop!*" If he heard me my warning failed to resonate. Instinct had dragged him to a dark place where only one thought got through—kill or be killed.

The land shark's blood soaked into the sand and stained Gabe-lion's muzzle a deep rust color. With one last twitch the massive fish fell to the ground—lifeless. Seconds later nothing remained but black tar.

Only then did Gabe glance up. His eyes blinked back to human. Pain and shock forced his change. "Celeste, I'm sorry. I ... I couldn't stop."

Blood loss quickly claimed its spoils. Gabe sat down hard in the sand, his skin ghostly pale and covered in blood. His head lolled to the side and his eyes rolled back. In a flap of feathers,

Kendall stood by his side, easing him to the ground and pouring healing warmth into him.

Icy prickles ran down my spine. Caleb wasn't with her.

I spun in a circle and found nothing except empty beach. The storm stilled as if holding its breath.

Caleb was ... *gone*. My breath came short and shallow. The world whipped around me like a crazy carnival ride. I didn't get to say goodbye. I deserved a split second to try to save him. How dare I be denied that? Lack of oxygen caused black spots to dance before my eyes. The ground rose up to meet me as my knees buckled.

I didn't even get a chance ...

A pair of arms caught me, manifesting out of black smoke. "Lovey! I'm here! I'm right here! It's okay!"

Grasping his shirt in tight fists, I clung hard to Caleb as my heart struggled to find its rhythm. I buried my face into his chest and desperately breathed in his scent. Despite his proclamation, things were far from okay. The universe just showed me how easily it could steal him from me. Nothing would ever be okay again.

CHAPTER EIGHT

The rocking chair creaked as I kept it in motion with one foot and stared out into the night. I rolled the piece of parchment paper Bernard gave me earlier between my fingers, but tried not to think about the words etched on it. Instead I focused on the snow, one flake at a time. I followed each one on its journey all the way to the ground before shifting my gaze to another. Shutting my brain off this way was mandatory. Only by keeping myself at an emotionally neutral state could I avoid the breakdown that threatened.

I quickly stuffed the paper in the pocket of my winter coat when the front door squeaked open.

Grams poked her head out, her thick zebra print throw blanket flung around her shoulders. "Sakes alive, Celeste! You'll catch your death out here! When you weren't at dinner I thought you'd gone to Caleb's."

"I was supposed to—" I pulled my phone out and checked the time. I had also missed four calls from him. "—an hour ago."

Grams chewed on that information for a moment. "And instead you've been out here this whole time?"

My chin quivered in betrayal as I nodded.

She took a seat in the rocker beside me before she asked, "Want to talk about it?"

I shook my head no but proceeded to unleash a geyser of emotion. "I thought I lost him today, Grams. For a split second, I thought I failed him. The tie needs to be broken so I can kill the

Titans. But if he's human he can't be around me. It's too dangerous. One second I think maybe it would be easier to know he's out there somewhere, safe. Then I hate myself for even entertaining the idea of giving up on him. But what are we doing now? We're fighting the inevitable. Sooner or later I'll swing too hard, or Gabe will lose control like he did today, and that'll be it. Either way, no matter what I do from this point on ... I'm going to lose him."

My whole body shook from the impact of the sobs I could no longer keep at bay. Grams scooted her chair closer and wrapped her arms around me. I rested my head on her shoulder and soaked her blanket with my tears.

"Oh, Celeste. I have no idea how you deal with half the bull that this calling of yours has thrown at you. I really don't." She stroked my hair and kissed the top of my head. "Yet you handle it with a grace and nobility that astounds me. I know I would've run for the hills a long time ago if I were in your shoes. The truth is, honey, other people may have all sorts of ideas about how you should live your life and handle your problems, but none of us—myself included—can know the stress and responsibility that rests solely on *you*."

I swiped at the tears with the back on my hand. "What do I do, Grams? Tell me, *please*. Because I can't make this decision. "

She used her thumb and forefinger to grab my chin and tip my face up toward hers. "Yes you can, and you will. Your heart will tell you what the right thing to do is, and you'll follow that. But you need to remember this; there's a reason *you* were chosen and not your brother or sister. Kendall, bless her heart, is all emotion. Gabe is pig-headed, but very passionate about his beliefs and opinions. Neither of them would be capable of what you are, and that's making the really tough decisions ... even when they hurt. That comes with inner strength, and *that* you have by the boatload. The right thing to do will come to you. You just have to be still and let your heart tell you what it is."

She released my chin and I nestled back onto her shoulder. I closed my eyes and let the tears flow free. As much as I hated to admit it, my heart already tried to tell me what I needed to do, but I purposely ignored it. I suspected I wouldn't like its answer.

☙ ✳ ❧

I called Caleb and blamed girl pains for my absence. As soon as we hung up I headed straight to bed. I just wanted to curl up under the covers and stay there until the house crumbled around me and grass grew over me.

I stepped into my bedroom and immediately noticed the scroll dressed in a red satin ribbon. My heart did a nervous flutter-beat as it beckoned from its perch on my pillow. If ever there was a moment that my mysterious ally needed to step up with some brilliantly insightful information, this was it. I crossed the room in three quick strides and scooped up the scroll. My hand hovered over the ribbon and shook. Fear caused me to hesitate. I sank down onto the edge of the bed and hugged the scroll to my chest. I counted to five then yanked the ribbon free before I chickened out. My hands trembled as I unrolled the thick paper. I held my breath as I read:

It's a sacrifice of love and one he would make for you if the roles were reversed.

A feeling I hadn't anticipated washed over me—certainty—followed by agonizing sorrow. I fell back on the bed, rolled onto my side, and curled my knees up to my chest. Since I learned of Caleb's link to the Titans I hadn't dared to ask myself the one question I needed to answer. How far would Caleb go to protect *me*? My heart spoke that answer without a shadow of a doubt.

How far would he go? *As far as it took.*

CHAPTER NINE

Shades of pink, yellow, and violet zigzagged across the sky like haphazard strokes from a paintbrush as the sunset over Ireland's gorgeous Cliffs of Moher. Their reflection cast a deep purple shade onto the water below that broke in a white spray at the base of the rocky cliffs. This truly was beauty defined.

Caleb slid his arms around my waist and nuzzled into the crook of my neck. "I told ya it was lovely."

I ran my hands down his arms and linked my fingers with his. "It's gorgeous. I can't believe I waited so long to let you bring me here."

Ebony hair tickled my cheek as he whispered in my ear, "Sometimes impendin' doom is just the kick in the pants ya need to arrange a long overdue holiday."

A harsh bucketful of icy reality doused all my warm snuggly feelings. We weren't here for a romantic rendezvous. I had a job to do. I pushed Caleb's arms away—much to his chagrin—and dug my phone out of my pocket to check the time.

"We've got about twenty minutes until the first phase begins. I need to start getting things ready."

The wood floor creaked under my feet as I strode to the knotty pine dresser to grab my satchel. Before I could get too far Caleb snagged my wrist and pulled me back to him. His fingers softly stroked my skin as he cupped my face in both his hands.

Nothing but love filled his gaze. "Thank ya, for what ya'r doin' for me today. Ya saved me from the Dark Army and now ya'r saving me from a burden I've beared for so long I ne'er dreamed I could be free of it. I'd heard of rituals like this, but thought they were fables shared between Dark Army orphans hopin' for a better life. But then I met you ... "

I grabbed his hands and gave them a quick squeeze before I pulled away. "Let's just hope it doesn't get you killed."

I turned my back to him before he could saw the pained grimace I struggled to hold back. Out of the same satchel that usually held my sketch book and art supplies came the ingredients that would alter my future forever. My chin threatened to quiver. Sheer determination refused to let it. First I removed the piece of parchment paper Bernard gave me with the precise instructions of what I had to do. After that came a vial of some weird, iridescent liquid, a tarnished silver goblet, a candle, matches, and what looked like a small bundle of sticks and leaves bound tightly together with string.

"Ya know I'm gonna be fine, lovey."

I glanced over my shoulder. Barefoot, with his hands stuffed in the pockets of his jeans and his blue flannel shirt untucked, he was a picture of calm relaxation. To him our worries and cares were an ocean away. I knew otherwise.

"That's why we came here, aye? You take that demon out of me and keep me safe from harm while ya'r brother and sister use those special weapons Bernard armed 'em with tah destroy the Titans once and for all." His shoulders rose and fell in a carefree shrug. "Way I see it, I'm safe as a wee babe with you as my body guard."

"Yeah, what could possibly go wrong?" Even I heard the bitterness of my tone.

In a puff of black smoke he stood beside me. He slipped a finger under my chin and tipped my face up so I had no choice but to stare into those hypnotizing emerald eyes. "Absolutely nothin'. I know my bein' human scares ya, but I'm not worried in the least. As long as I'm with you, everything else will work out."

"I hope so." I swallowed hard to dislodge the lump in my throat, then changed the subject with a nod at the incantation ingredients. "We need to get started."

"Aye. What can I do tah help?"

I struck a match and lit the candle. "Empty that vial into the goblet."

Caleb popped the cap off and peeked inside as he swirled the shimmering liquid around. "It looks like dish soap." He sniffed it and cringed. "Phew! It does *not* smell like it."

"Then I'd suggest plugging your nose when you drink it." I used the same match to light my bushel of leaves and sticks. They sizzled and smoked. Their earthy smell quickly filled the room. I shook the match to extinguish it.

Caleb crossed the room and yanked the window open a crack. "I have tah drink that vile smellin' stuff? I grew up on a demon plane, but that *smells* evil."

I waved my smoldering sticks in small circles around the goblet. "Yep, that's considered your consent to break the bond."

A smile tugged at the corners of his mouth. "Makes sense, I guess. Ya have tah want it badly enough to drink liquefied cow dung. That's how they rule out those that only kinda wanna be human."

That garnered a genuine laugh despite my somber mood. "Well, it's about that time, sir. Cow dung or not, bottoms up."

His hand closed around the base of the goblet. Pain the likes of which I'd never known seized my heart. He swirled the blue liquid around causing a tiny bit to slosh out. I watched him raise the cup to his lips as if he moved in slow motion. When that liquid touched his tongue everything would change. He'd never know I lied to him. He'd never know how much this hurt me. I wanted to scream for him to stop. To knock the cup from his hands before it was too late and get lost in his arms forever. Instead I stood silent and promised myself that somehow, someway we would be together again.

He poured the liquid into his mouth and my breath caught. There was no going back now.

"Gah! That was horrid!" He slammed the now empty goblet down onto the dresser with more force than necessary. "That's it now, isn't it? Restored mortality comin' up?"

My words came out breathless and forced, "When the moon is at its highest the bond will be broken."

And you'll be gone.

A wide smile of genuine happiness spread across his face. "No reason the celebration can't start now, aye? I'll get a cozy fire goin' in the fireplace, we'll crack open the bottle of wine I brought—because ya'r of legal drinkin' age here in lovely Ir'land— then we'll toast my last night as a demon and the beginnin' of our *human* life together." He hooked his hand around the back of my neck and pulled me close for a quick kiss, then darted off whistling.

I pressed the back of my hand to my mouth and watched him work. How do you act normal when it feels like your world just imploded? Was it possible to go through the motions of normalcy when all I wanted to do was lay down and cry? This wasn't the first time I had pondered that question. Right after Daddy died I asked Grams how we could possibly go on without him. She had swiped at her own tears with a handkerchief and answered, "We'll keep breathing, keep moving, and trust time to do its job and heal our hearts."

I let the memory of those words resonate through me and tried to steady my breath. I forced one foot in front of the other all the way to the weathered rocking chair by the fireplace. My gaze stayed locked on Caleb. I wanted to memorize every inch of him, to be able to recall even the subtlest nuances. The strong line of his jaw. That wonderful area just below his hairline on the back of his neck that I found so soft and touchable. How his silky hair felt when I ran it between my fingers. How right it felt when his strong arms pulled me in close …

"Celeste? Are ya listenin' tah a word I'm sayin', lovey?"

I expelled a breath I hadn't realized I'd been holding. "No. I really wasn't," I admitted with the best flirty smirk I could manage. It felt so awkward and uncomfortable I could only imagine it made me look constipated. "I was busy admiring the view."

He scooted across the floor and knelt beside my chair. "I know ya'r troubled, love. And I know why. But I need ya tah know that I'm gonna be okay. If I died tomorrow it wouldn't be a loss. Not for me. Because I have you." He gently pressed his palm to my face and used his thumb to wipe away the lone tear that snuck down my cheek. "Ya'r all I want, and all I'll e'er need. And even though me being human scares ya, it thrills me tah no end. Because now we have a chance at a real life together. One I couldn't have offered ya before."

Caleb's hand hovered over mine. Black smoke puffed in the space between them. I glanced down at my hand while Caleb shifted his position. My mouth fell open. A diamond solitaire set between two emeralds had materialized on the ring finger of my left hand.

NO! My brain screamed. *This can't be what I think it is, because that's too painful for* any *person to bear!*

The raven-haired soon-to-be ex-demon dropped to one knee before me and took my hand. There were words. Wonderfully, sweet words that I couldn't hear over the sound of my heart breaking. His traditional ending of, "Celeste Marie Garrett, will ya marry me?" stabbed into my heart like a hooked dagger meant not only to puncture, but to rip the beating muscle right from my chest.

Tears streaked down my cheeks in torrents and blurred my vision. Fate served as a wicked enchantress with a twisted and cruel sense of humor yet tonight I refused to let her win. Tomorrow my life would be a shattered mess from which I may never recover. But on *this* night I planned to act on my desires—with no regrets.

"Yes," I hiccupped and fell into his arms.

The sensual caress of his hair against my cheek awoke a passionate urgency in me. I needed the contact of his skin on mine more than I had ever needed anything in my life. My desire awoke with a vengeance and I hungrily brought my lips to his.

Caleb caught my face and pulled back, questions written all over his face. "Love, ya'r tremblin'."

A lone thought sparked in my mind and built in intensity like a raging wildfire. I peered deep into the gaze of the man I loved—*my fiancé*.

"Make love to me." My voice didn't waver at this request.

Caleb ran his fingers through my hair. A sweet smile softened his lips. "As much as I'd love to—and believe me I would—if I want ya'r Grams tah continue tah like me I have tah at least suggest we wait until we're actually married. We've waited this long, what's a few more months, aye?"

I scooted off the rocking chair and settled on to his lap with my legs wrapped around him. Only a veil of electricity separated my lips from his. "In my next life I'll wait. I can't in this one."

Our mouths met with mutual need. Everything we had, everything we were, we offered to each other. In a puff of smoke we crossed the room. The mattress squeaked softly when Caleb eased me down on to it. I fumbled with the buttons of his shirt, my quaking hands unable to thumb them free. He yanked the bothersome garment over his head and tossed it across the room. My fingers traced across the intricate Celtic pattern branded on his chest, over the crisscrossed scars from countless battles, down those chiseled abs, and finally hooked over the waistband of his jeans.

Despite the hunger in his eyes, Caleb caught my hand. His voice came out a breathless growl. "Are ya sure this is what ya want, lovey?"

I said nothing, but let the snap as I unfastened his jeans answer for me. I had no doubts. Before I lost him forever, I would have all of him.

CHAPTER TEN

Silky, soft sand slid between my toes. Not a single cloud marred the brilliant blue sky. Sunlight streamed down and warmed my skin with its kiss. A faint breeze lifted my hair and made it dance across my bare shoulders. The sides of my hair were pulled up and pinned with a few brightly colored flowers; the orange Tiger Lily was my favorite. I shifted my bouquet—yellow, fuchsia, orange, and white lilies set against a bed of green ivy— into my right hand. With my free hand I smoothed my dress one last time. The loose, flowing fabric stopped just below my knee. Its empire cut design and thin spaghetti straps made it simple, elegant, and perfect for me. Daddy extended his arm. I happily hooked my own around it. Flecks of gold glimmered in his chestnut eyes as he beamed at me. I smiled back and gave his arm a squeeze.

In the distance, a guitar strummed softly.

"That's our cue. You ready, Cee-Cee?" Daddy asked and closed his hand over mine.

I took a deep breath of the salty sea air and exhaled slowly. "More than I've ever been ready for anything my entire life."

"Let's go then." He winked.

Ahead of us an aisle awaited sprinkled with rose petals and lined with white folding chairs that held all my friends and family. They turned in their seats as we began our processional. Smiles followed us up the aisle. My heart fluttered in my chest when I saw his silhouette under the floral archway. The turquoise ocean lapped its sweet serenade behind him, yet I marveled at Caleb's beauty. The sun glistened off his ebony locks. A golden glow brightened his skin. He wore a white buttoned-down shirt left untucked with the sleeves rolled up and khaki slacks rather than a tux. His feet were bare, just like mine.

Daddy kissed me on the cheek, placed my hand gently in Caleb's, and took his seat beside Mom. A tear slid from his eye and Mom laid her hand on his knee to comfort him.

"Dearly beloved," a harsh voice began. My head whipped around. Presiding over our nuptials was the Grand Councilwoman, the same gruff and unforgiving woman that had stripped Alaina of her powers and saddled me with my own little gnome of doom. Her gown of raven feathers covered all but her hands and pinched face. The feathers on her head were pulled tightly back in a makeshift bun. "We are gathered here today to join this man and this woman in Holy Matrimony ... "

I glanced at Caleb. While my smile had vanished his held firm, seemingly undisturbed by her presence. Behind me Kendall and Alaina wore matching blue sundresses and content smiles. Gabe stood in the best man position with his hands behind his back and a warm grin on his face. Everyone seemed okay with this, except me. I shook my head then shifted my focus back to the glorious moment at hand.

"At this time the Groom would like to recite the traditional Celtic vows to his bride." The Councilwoman gestured for him to proceed with a bird-like jerk of her head.

Alaina stepped forward with a yellow cord. She wrapped it first around Caleb's hand and then around mine.

"Handfasting. It's a Celtic tradition," she whispered with a soft smile then returned to her place in line.

Caleb cleared his throat and began, his voice strong and assertive. "I vow to you the first cut of meat, the first sip of wine. From this day on it shall be only your name I cry out in the night and into your eyes that I shall smile each morning."

A wave crashed against the shore. Odd on such a calm and fair weathered day. I glanced up. Grey clouds moved in fast and the water churned angrily.

"I shall be a shield for your back as you are mine," a deep resonate boom of a voice said, and I snapped my head around.

The Gryphon stood in Caleb's place.

The cord that tied my hand to the talon of the towering creature was all that prevented me from tumbling to the ground in shock. His lion torso rippled with muscle. Flaxen feathers covered his face and neck. His beak curled down into a sharp and deadly point. The wide, powerful shape of his head and pointed ears looked more lion-like than eagle. Majestic wings arched up behind him, making his formidable appearance that much more daunting.

"Nor shall a grievous word be spoken about us, for our marriage is sacred between us and no stranger shall hear my grievance. Above and beyond this, I will cherish and honor you through this life and into the next."

I didn't want to be bonded to him, not like this. I sought out the faces of my loved ones and silently pleaded for someone to help me. My mother swiped at her tears with a lacy handkerchief. Daddy gave me a warm grin and a reassuring nod. From Grams I got a jovial thumbs up. Even my brother and sister—my sword and my shield—smiled their approval.

Lightning flashed overhead as sky opened up and dumped torrential rains down by the bucketful. All the wedding guests shrieked and ran for cover. The only bodies left on the beach belonged to me ... and my betrothed.

A third voice picked up where the previous one left off, "Ye are blood of my blood, and bone of my bone." Rain blurred my vision. I swiped at my face with my free hand to see if the impossible was true. She was—me. Not me exactly, but a version of. For starters regular me wouldn't be caught dead in the frayed and revealing animal skin outfit she wore. Her skin was covered with dirt and what appeared to be soot. A long, thick braid hung down her back. Blue painted symbols and markings decorated her bare arms and lined her cheeks. I didn't have to wonder who she was. I'd met her before, just not face-to-face. She lived in me as the Celtic warrior fate demanded I be. "I give ye my body, that we two might be one. I give ye my spirit, 'til our life shall be done."

A choked sob tore from my throat. Caleb had been the dream. A distraction. From the start we could never have worked because of my tie to another. Tears streamed down my face. Their traces—as well as any hope I clung to—washed away by the rain.

The warrior's dirt-stained fingers dug into my skin to the point of pain. She grasped my forearm and yanked me closer. Her other hand balled into a fist that she thumped against her chest and held over her heart. Outwardly her eyes projected a mirror image of my own. Yet hers held no pain—just the absolute resolution that comes with duty, honor, and responsibility. I envied her battle-hardened heart. It seemed an improvement over my own that lay crumpled in my chest, shattered beyond repair. I coveted her existence for its simplicity—an option life refused to give me. Not yet anyway. I attempted to embrace her uncomplicated existence by clasping my hand around her arm and returning her salute while the rain poured down.

ଔ ✳ ଇ

I woke up alone. The bed beside me long since cold, but still smelled of him. The room that last night provided a cozy little love nest now felt as frigid and isolated as a prison cell. I swung my feet over the side of the bed and dragged myself to the window. The world outside looked too bright. Too green. Like a manic fairy tale in Tim Burton's imagination. The curtain rattled across its rod as I pulled it shut. I returned to the bed and curled myself around the pillow where Caleb slept next to me for the first and last time. That's when the first round of tears broke free. With wrenching sobs that shook the bed with their force my misery came pouring out.

CHAPTER ELEVEN

I didn't ask where Bernard had taken me. Frankly, I didn't care. He came to get me in Ireland with the plan of throwing me into the middle of a Titan smorgasbord. The locale he blinked us to turned out to be a desolate, wind lashed dune.

Gabe, still in human form, was clad only in a pair of faded jeans. The muscles across his chest and back flexed as he swung a long-handled double-sided axe at a fire demon. The ax severed the creature's head from its body. Ash rained down and covered Gabe with a layer of grey over his bare skin. One down, eleven more to go. Three of fire, two Bat-bulls, four of the sparky lightning dudes, and two land sharks that were snapping their teeth and circling Kendall on their stubby little leg nubbins. Most days I would've found the crowd of demons around my loved ones worrisome. At that moment, I couldn't muster that emotion—or any other.

A mace dangled from Kendall's delicate hand as she held the tips of her extended wings in close enough to protect her. From the way she was held it—like it might contaminate her—I sincerely doubted she had swung it even once.

"Those are the other enchanted weapons?" I jerked my head at the axe and mace as I fastened the sheathed broadsword Bernard gave me around my hips.

The fat little gnome dug his cane into the sand to lean on it. "Yes. The Council forged them for you specifically to use against the Titans. They are drawn to the instruments like moths to a flame. Just like that flame to that moth, the weapons are incredibly deadly."

"All I need to know," I muttered and marched across the sand. I ducked, twirled, and weaved through the demons, locked on my destination.

Kendall's head snapped around when my left hand closed over the heavy metal handle of the mace. Her platinum hair bounced as she peered from my hand to my face and back again. Relief registered a split second before her eyebrows raised in surprise. "Celeste! Wow, nice ring! Where'd you get it?"

I took a deep breath and let it out slowly. Wordlessly I readjusted my grip on the weapon.

Comprehension widened her eyes. Her mouth formed a perfect O. "Oh. Oh *no*. Do you want to talk about it?"

"Nope. Gabe, get her out of here!" I shoved past Kendall and walloped a land shark in the head with the spikes of the mace. Bone crunched. Its teeth snapped one more time before it flopped to the ground and darkened the sand by turning to black ooze.

Gabe said nothing, just gave me a sympathetic lift of his chin before handing over the axe. He grabbed Keni's upper arm, found an opening, and maneuvered them both out of the circle of demons.

I weighed both weapons in my hands to get the feel of them.

"Wa ... wait!" Keni protested and tried to plant her feet in the sand. "We have to help her!"

The Titans encircled me with a wall of electrically charged, earth trembling, teeth gnashing, heat. I kept my gaze cast down but turned my head to one side and then the other to crack my neck.

Keni shook free of Gabe's grasp and reeled toward me. "We can't leave her alone!"

Gabe caught her around the waist and hoisted her over his shoulder like a sack of potatoes. "Yes, we can. She's got this. Call it butt-kicking therapy."

I couldn't have said it better myself. I brought my head up as the first demon—the other land shark looking for a little payback—attacked. I whipped the mace over my head and brought it down into the shark's belly. With a *huff* it toppled over. Going with the momentum, I spun on a rapidly approaching grey-skinned Sparky dude. This time I opted for the axe and severed his legs at the knee. His black lips curled back from rotted teeth as he screamed and fell to the ground. Sparks shot from his fingers while he writhed in the sand. Before I could finish him off, a lasso of fire circled the wrist of my axe wielding hand and yanked it back. My skin scorched, but I didn't loosen my grip. Instead I swung the mace with every ounce of strength I had. His flaming skull splintered and he crumbled into ash. The rancid breath of the charging Bat-bulls stung my nostrils. I responded by twisting into a low kick. One got his legs knocked out from under him while his friend took an axe to the gut. For good measure, I went ahead and relieved the downed Bat-bull of his head.

Ash blew through the air as I rose to my feet among the carnage. Four remained. Three lightning, and one rather nervous looking fire demon.

"You seem hesitant." Ash scorched my throat and turned my voice into a deep growl even I didn't recognize. "Maybe you'd like it if we evened the odds a little bit?"

I flung the axe behind me without even a backward glance. It embedded between the eyes of the injured lightning demon with a sickening *thunk*.

Kendall grimaced. "Well, that was gross and unnecessary."

The desire for my blood reached a feverish level for the three remaining lightning demons. Anger sparked from them in a visible charge. The fire demon, however, inched away. His empty eye sockets were fixated on the broad sword on my hip.

I reached across my body and pulled the blade out just enough to expose the shine of its metal. "Is this what's bothering you? Think I need to lose this one, too?"

His flaming bone skull tilted to the side. Daring me. Taunting me. Then he slowly nodded.

"Fair enough." The sword hissed out of the leather holster and winged through the air. A fresh round of ash exploded as the deadly steel sliced the fire demon's skull in two.

"Nice!" Gabe marveled.

"That wasn't nice!" Keni squealed and shielded her eyes. "That was, like, the exact opposite of nice!"

Blue electricity snapped around me. The last three demons moved in wearing identical sneers. The Dark Army must teach a class to achieve such precision—Sneering 101. I took a deep breath and embraced all the pain and agony festering inside me. I owned it. Let it rule me. Then swung. A scream tore from my chest as I lashed the mace through all three of them with one superhuman strike. The mace entered the rib cage of the first, and exited the shoulder blade of the last.

Ash danced in the wind. The demons' lifeless bodies slumped to the ground and dissolved into goo. My chest rose and fell as I surveyed the remnants of my slaughter. I knew it was twisted, but I was sad it was over. The momentary reprieve I had hoped this would provide never came.

The mace slid from my fingers and thumped into the sand. " ... And then there were none."

CHAPTER TWELVE

I had a key to this particular door, but raised my hand to knock anyway. Before my fist made contact with the sage green door it flew open. A disheveled Rowan leaned against the frame. His golden hair was a ruffled mess, his black shirt completely unbuttoned. The dirty jeans he wore hung low enough to reveal the rise of his hipbones.

"Well, if it isn't the Black Widow," he slurred. "A lad falls for you and then disappears into oblivion." He tipped up a long-necked beer bottle and poured the amber liquid into his mouth then wiped his lips with the back of his hand. "Guess I should thank you for choosing him over me, aye?"

"I take it you heard."

His hair fell across his forehead in a way that gave him an air of approachability—like a little boy. Of course his personality counteracted that right quick.

"Heard? No." He leaned forward as if to whisper a secret but failed to lower his voice. "We demons can sometimes sense each other. And yesterday I was just sitting around, minding me own business," beer sloshed out of the bottle as he gestured with it, "entertaining myself with a very lovely and flexible gymnast, when—*poof*! I actually felt Cal vanish. One second his presence is there, the next gone without a trace." He pointed at me with the top of his beer bottle. "I'm guessing *you* had everything to do with that."

"You know exactly what I did and why." I crinkled my nose. "Are you aware you smell like a brewery?"

Rowan pushed off the doorframe and stumbled back into the apartment. I assumed the fact that he left the door wide open acted as my invitation to enter.

"There's a very good reason for that. You see, in between plotting your doom and mourning the loss of me mate, I've been reacquainting myself with the wonders of ale. It's a wonderful beverage. I really don't know why the Countess prohibits it."

I stepped inside and froze. Caleb's black motorcycle jacket with the silver stripes down the sleeves hung on a hook in the hall. My breath caught. If Rowan wasn't there I probably would've ripped that thing off the wall, thrown it on the ground, and rolled around on it like a dog just because it smelled like Caleb.

I blinked hard to regain focus. "You've been plotting my doom?"

Rowan pushed an empty pizza box aside to allow himself room to collapse on the ugly plaid couch. "Aye. Since you took away the closest thing I've had to family in centuries, I've thought of little else than how to properly pay ya back. But as I'm currently seein' three of you, it may not be the best time to act on such impulses. I'd hate to kill the wrong one and anger the other two."

I cleared off a spot amongst the beer bottles and food wrappers to sit down on the dark oak coffee table. With my elbows resting on my knees I leaned toward Rowan. "And what if I were to tell you I came here to ask for your help?"

The pretty-boy pirate nearly choked on his beer. He sat up a second before it came out of his nose. "I'd say my days of helping *you* passed about forty-eight hours ago. Unless you have a nagging death wish I can help with. As soon as I sleep this off I would *gladly* help with that."

"No. Actually I have an idea that would make *both* of us feel better."

Rowan ran his fingers through his hair and attempted a leer that probably would've been sexy about seven beers ago. "Oh ... I see what this is."

"I really don't think you do."

He leaned *way* too far into my personal space to reach around me—so close that his hair tickled my cheek. I flinched and backed away, mostly from the beer stench. When he pulled back he had a remote in his hand and used it to click the stereo to life. Maroon 5 flooded the room proudly proclaiming their Jagger-like moves.

Rowan bit his lower lip and bobbed to the music. "Boyfriend's barely gone two days and already you need a rebound tumble? Much as I hate you, I might be *just* drunk enough for that."

I snatched the remote from him and rounded the table in a flash to snap the radio off. Distance between Mr. Rebound and me suddenly seemed crucial. "Whoa! There will be no tumbling!"

"Your loss," he muttered with a noncommittal shrug.

I inhaled a cleansing breath and tried another approach with the obtuse pirate—the blatant, ugly truth. "Okay, here's the thing. I can't breathe. Can't ... think. With Caleb gone I'm ... broken." I stared down at my hands and fiddled with my ring. The hole through my center caused by the loss of him began to gush, spewing its painful nastiness everywhere. I couldn't stop it if I tried. "I know you miss him, Rowan. He was your brother and I took him from you. For that I am so, so sorry. You have to believe me when I say I was trying to protect him. As much as it hurts, I can live knowing he's out there somewhere, safe. But if he stayed and got killed because of me, because of what I am, I couldn't live with that. If you need to hate me, I can accept that. Hell, *I* hate me right now. But I'm asking you to put that aside and help me. Please. I have a job to do, a pretty friggin' important one. But I can't function to do it when all I can think about is how much I miss him."

My chin quivered, but I clenched my jaw and refused to let myself cry in front of him. "It's literally killing me. I'm asking you to please take it away. Just for a little while. Use your ability to give me a few moments peace. Please?"

My plea seemed to clear away a bit of his fog. Clarity sharpened those turquoise eyes. He rose from the couch and walked to me. His arms hung to his sides in a pointed message that he had no intention of giving me what I yearned for. "And why would I help you? Give me one reason not to let you stew in your own misery. Because from where I'm standing, poppet, you deserve to."

I squared my shoulders and met his gaze directly. "Because I'm the only one that can give it back to you."

His forehead creased in confusion. "What?"

"Do you remember on Liberty Island? The urgency to get to Caleb? I gave you that. I'm empathic."

Rowan's head tipped back. He gazed at me down the bridge of his nose. A blend of hope and doubt swirled in his eyes.

"I know you're hurting. But you can't use your mind control on yourself to dull the pain." I jabbed my thumb at the bottles strewn everywhere. "Hence the drinking binge. But if you help me—offer me a little relief—I can give it back to you. We can both get a temporary reprieve from our emotion."

Rowan stood silent, a maneuver I didn't know him to be capable of. His face went slack from any and all emotion. No one can manage a poker face like a drunken pirate. The wait lingered on long enough that I began to anticipate him telling me where I could shove my empathic ability while he cracked another beer.

Then, his hand closed around mine. For the first time since waking up alone in Ireland the pain eased and I could breathe.

Part Two

CHAPTER THIRTEEN

Six months later

I unsheathed my dragon's tooth dagger in mid-stride and twirled the blade around my fingers once before letting the mother of pearl grip settle into my grasp.

"Great job on that Kepac demon, Celeste, but there are two more up ahead," Bernard's voice chimed in my head, a fun little spell he used to make my fights more efficient.

Between a Gryphon who read my mind at will and a gnome that chattered away in my brain my head felt like a very crowded place as of late.

"Gabe has one pinned. Kendall is doing her best to keep the other at bay. They're right on the border of town, so keep this fight tight and quiet."

"No sweat, Bernie." I pumped my arms and zigzagged through the trees. He wasn't kidding about being close to town. Through the break in the trees I could see the parking lot lights of Big Al's Grocery Store.

I swiped at a wall of foliage with my readied blade and broke into the scene of the battle. A barrel roll over Gabe-lion's back got me into position to shove Kendall aside and sink the dagger into the belly of the Kepac.

"Thanks, Cee," she murmured and wiped the sweat from her brow with the back of her arm. "I couldn't have kept him off Gabe much longer."

"No worries." I shrugged and tucked the dagger into the back waistband of my cut-off sweats. The balmy Tennessee summer required a "less is more" philosophy for fighting attire.

I nudged Gabe's tawny hide with my knee. Topaz feline eyes flicked my way and a challenging snarl rumbled through his teeth.

"Easy, kitty. You know the drill."

Gabe huffed, but relented. He kept his weight on the demon until I stepped up, put my foot on its throat and called on my telekinesis to pin its body to the ground. A nod to Gabe and he slunk off to scour the darkness for any further threats.

I tilted my head and peered down at my captive. FYI, Kepac demons? Not cute. They're known for their lower lip that's roughly the size of a dinner plate and has a rhinoceros tusk jutting out of it. That's a hard flaw to look past.

Its ghostly pallor went from red to purple. I eased the pressure a bit and it hungrily gulped the air. Panic widened his solid black eyes.

"Celeste, you need to ... "

I purposely cut off my mind gnome's anticipated words. "Do you know about the new force rising?"

Saliva dripped from the corners of its wide fish mouth. "People vanishing. New demons being made."

"No idea who's behind it? Or where to find them?" I had a very good idea ... Alec. But my efforts to keep him safe relied on the Dark Army *not* figuring that out.

He shook his head as much as he was able. "None. The Countess is searching. She wants whoever's behind it dead. Immediately."

I fought to keep my expression neutral despite my alarm that Alec had put himself on the Countess's radar. To keep him alive and cure him of whatever evil infected him, I *had* to find him before she did. Unfortunately, I had run out of places to look.

I shifted my foot slightly to dig the tread of my shoe in a little more. "And what about me? What new form of torment does your boss have on the docket?"

Its eyes bulged with terror. It wasn't fear of *me* that prompted this reaction but the idea of betraying a woman viewed to have endless power and resources.

I squatted down and rocked a bit more of my weight on the foot that held him. It struggled to suck in a breath as its coloring transitioned to blue.

"Because of the Countess I lost the man that I love," I whispered. "She's not the only one you should fear. I'm six degrees of angry and would love a violent outlet for it. However, unlike her, *I* can show mercy. *If* you cooperate. If you don't … "

I let my words trail off with the obvious threat, and then rose to my feet and eased the pressure. I gave it time to suck in a few breaths before staring down with an expectant stare.

"Your … inner … circle … has … been … breached," the Kepac gasped. "Don't trust … "

I hadn't moved or flinched, but suddenly the demon omitted a choked gurgle. Its black eyes rolled back in its head, leaving only white voids. I released it completely and took a step back. The creature's body jerked spastically, flopping against the ground like a fish out of water. Foamy spittle bubbled on his lips. One final shudder and it went limp.

Keni stepped up beside me. Her nose crinkled as the demon turned to ooze. "That's one way to shut up a minion."

I spun around as my lion sentry trotted up and gave a nod that the perimeter was secured. "She keeps a tight watch on her soldiers. The puppet was about to say something its master didn't like. Still didn't hurt to ask though." I glanced back over my shoulder at the tar-like substance that had recently been a living, breathing creature with an unfortunate lip condition. "Well, didn't hurt *us* to ask … "

"So are we done here?" Keni clapped her hands. Her blue eyes were sparkling with delight. "I want to head home and get some sleep. Grams is taking us to Bed, Bath, and Beyond in the morning, and she's going to let me decorate the guest room for when Mom gets into town!"

"Bernie?" I knew I looked crazy talking to myself, but at least my siblings knew it to be magic related and not a mental health issue. "Kepacs have been eliminated, no further threat in sight."

Even in my head, a mouthful of berries garbled his words. "Great job, Celeste. Very impressive. Feel free to head home and rest up."

A sizzle of static indicated he severed the connection. He left me with only the sound of my inner monologue in my head.

I paused for a moment, nodded, and gave an, "Okay, will do," to no one. I met my brother and sister's inquiring gazes directly and didn't bat an eye as the lie left my tongue. "Bernard said you two can head home. He wants me to do one more quick sweep."

CB✳BO

Astride Caleb's motorcycle I rode at break neck speeds, zooming around the few cars that cruised along the highway this late at night. The bike purred beneath me as the highway lights blurred past.

About thirty minutes after the battle, I eased the bike into the gravel driveway, my urgency grew with every second that ticked by. I parked, yanked off my helmet and raced up the stairs in a blur of superhuman speed.

Rowan met me at the door. The tight-lipped smile he wore in no way hid his annoyance. He gestured for me to enter with a grand wave of his arm.

"Bad time?" I didn't really care, but it seemed polite to ask.

One corner of his mouth pulled back in a wry grin. "No, *Mo Chroi*. After the incident with the cheerleader I've learned not to have visitors or plans of any kind this time of night."

Mo Chroi, his fun little nickname for me. Gaelic for my burden. Caleb had taught it to him years ago. The irony of it wasn't lost on me.

"It's not my fault she couldn't take a joke." I stepped into the apartment and closed the door behind me.

"Of course." He raked a hand through his messy hair. I must've gotten him out of bed; he was dressed in a fitted white t-shirt and black cotton pajama pants. "Because sorry your date with the football team got cancelled couldn't be taken as anything *but* a joke."

Normally I would've had a witty comeback for that, yet that persistent ache in my gut made it impossible for me to think of anything except my need for relief.

"Do you mind?" I nodded toward his bedroom.

Concern seeped into his turquoise eyes and his lips pressed together in a firm line. "You didn't even attempt to fall asleep alone tonight did you?"

I stared at my tennis shoes and shook my head.

He opened his mouth to say something, and then reconsidered with a shrug. "Beautiful woman wants to climb into my bed? Who am I to refuse her?"

With that he turned and strode down the hallway to his room.

I kicked off my shoes and followed him. For just a moment I paused outside Caleb's door. Many times I had tortured myself by sitting on his bed, surrounded by the possessions he left behind—*just like me*. No good came of that. Tonight I forced myself to keep walking, straight down the hall to Rowan's room.

I entered to find Rowan throwing back the covers of his rumpled, unmade bed. He stood back, giving me a silent invitation to settle in.

I climbed onto the bed and rolled toward the door with my knees curled up to my chest. My teeth chattered in anticipation. Anxiously I fiddled with the ring that still adorned my left hand. Soon, relief would come.

Rowan pulled the covers over me and scooted up beside me. His hand hovered over the surface of my skin—wandering over my hand, up to my elbow, back down to my wrist, and up again—but he hesitated to touch me. I tilted my face toward him to see what the hold-up was. Was that a flicker of uncertainty? For a moment he looked almost … vulnerable. The moment disappeared as fast as it appeared. His go-to expression of detached arrogance returned and he slapped his hand down on my shoulder.

I nestled back onto the pillow that smelled of his citrus shampoo. The effects of his touch were instantaneous. Waves of relaxation washed over me; seeping into the hole that burned in me and temporarily patching my wounds. A blanket of calming energy settled over me.

"Do you need me to give it back?" Even I heard the audible drowsiness in the slow drag of my words.

"No. Not tonight." Rowan eased himself down on the pillow beside me, but didn't break his hold.

My blinks became longer. "Will you teleport me home if I fall asleep?"

"I always do, *Mo Chroi*."

"Rowan? Do you miss it?"

"Miss what?"

I yawned. "The pirate life."

"Aye. I miss the sea. She holds a powerful draw." Deep longing crept into his voice. He stared up at the ceiling, lost in thought—undoubtedly transported by memory to far off lands that I never even imagined. "When there's nothin' before ya but sky, water, and endless possibility. It's a freedom only the sea provides. A true freedom. One that beckons to me every second of every day."

"Sounds amazing," I murmured as I fell asleep, longing for that kind of freedom.

CHAPTER FOURTEEN

Most people would quit a job after their arch nemesis masqueraded as their boss and tried to kill their entire family. Unfortunately, since being the Chosen One only pays in emotional scars and a killer right jab, I held onto my job at the Neighborhood Café. Odds were slim the Dark Army would try the same trick twice. However, I still intended to watch the staff carefully for signs of odd "oops I just got possessed by an evil sorceress" type behavior—just in case.

The quaint little shop sat across the street from Nashville Community College—where I formerly studied art—and it fulfilled the co-eds needs for caffeine and an inexpensive dining option. Business was booming thanks to the new manager, my friend Sophia. Sophia happened to be a muse originally sent by the Council to motivate me to date. Yep, I'm *that* kind of pathetic. Unfortunately she took the blame for me falling for a half-demon and they terminated her position. Thanks to the muse trait of always taking things in stride, Sophia simply redirected her energies into motivating the café customers to buy stuff. Now the place bustled with activity from open to close.

I wiped off one of our bistro style tables and seated the next customers. With their order fresh on my pad, I rounded the counter and handed it to Sophia to fill.

"You're out early tonight, right?" She poured a cup of coffee and set it on my tray. "To get stuff ready for your Mom's visit?"

"Yep." I grabbed a napkin and swabbed up the droplets of coffee she'd spilt on the counter. "She comes into town tomorrow."

She grabbed two chocolate chip cookies with a plastic gloved hand and plated them for my customers. "Why don't you sound more excited? When's the last time you saw her?"

"Christmas, and I *am* excited, just not looking forward to running supernatural interference."

Sophia's almond-shaped brown eyes sparked with interest. "Want me to distract her for you? She's not seeing anyone, is she? 'Cause I could arrange ... "

My eyebrows shot up and I raised one finger. "Ah! None of that! I don't want you ... *inspiring* her in any way, shape, or form. Got it? That's my mom. You encouraging her to get freaky is icky."

Her full lips drooped into a pout. She flipped her head and whipped her long, mahogany braid over her shoulder. "Party pooper."

We both glanced up when the door chimed yet again. Instead of a customer, it turned out to be a rosy cheeked Kendall whose hair was a wind-blown mess. "Hey, Cee!"

"Uh ... Keni, how did you get here?" I had a feeling I already knew the answer, but sincerely hoped I was wrong.

She glanced around at the crowded room then mouthed the words. "I flew."

I leaned over the counter, ready to grab her and deliver a much needed head-butt. "Kendall, it's the middle of the day!" Even she couldn't misconstrue the urgency of my hissed whisper.

Her ocean blue eyes rolled. "Chillax, Cee. I totally stayed out of sight! After all this time I know enough to fly just below the clouds so no one sees me."

Sophia and I exchanged matching wide-eyed, tight-lipped expressions.

Mentally I counted to ten. "Just *below* the clouds?"

"Yeah!" Her blonde locks bobbed as she nodded. "Then no one can see me because I'm blocked by the—" the sudden understanding made her cheerful expression drop like a lead weight, "—ohhhhh."

I ran a hand over my face and tried to think of a plausible explanation to give Bernard about a possible outbreak of angel sightings.

Sophia laid a comforting hand on my shoulder and addressed Keni with a warm smile. "What was it you needed, honey?"

"Gabe took Grams' Buick to get the brakes fixed. So we need to borrow the truck to go get the supplies to make the centerpieces. I'm gonna decoupage *the crap* out of some stuff." Keni bounced on the balls of her feet and clapped in excitement … over arts and crafts. How did we come from the same womb?

I snatched my purse from my cubby below the counter, all the while biting the inside of my cheek to suppress the snarky comments that wanted so badly to leap from my mouth. I managed to keep them at bay as I dug my keys out then dangled them from my index finger. When Keni reached for them I yanked them away from her hand. "From now on we fly … "

She tsked. "Just *above* the clouds."

"And what don't we do in my truck?"

Keni jammed one fist onto her cocked hip. "Come on, Cee! *Seriously*?"

She could give me that look all she wanted. It was *my* truck. Whining would get her nowhere but walking. "What don't we do?"

"We don't drive and text." She *harrumphed*.

Reluctantly, I handed over my keys. "Actually I was going for we don't mess with my radio but yeah, don't do that either."

"Hurry home and you can be in charge of gluing!" Keni promised—or threatened—then bounced out the door.

An amused smile curled Sophia's lips as she watched Keni go. "Bet you'll be happy when all this wedding stuff is over." Back on task, she slid the tea on my tray to complete the order. "Only one more week of bachelorette parties, rehearsal dinners, and hall decorating before the main attraction."

An image flashed through my mind of a certain wedding on a beach that would never be.

"The sooner it's over the better," I mumbled, then balanced the tray on my hand and weaved my way to the table to deliver it. I was reaching down, handing a long-haired student with Buddy Holly glasses his coffee, when the bell over the door chimed again.

I glanced up, my smile fixed, ready to utter the customary, "Hi, we'll be right with you." Those words lodged in my throat at the sight of ebony hair that cast faint shades of blue under the café lights. A green flannel shirt peeked out from under a black leather jacket.

He found his way back. He remembers.

The coffee cup slipped from my hand, bounced off the table, and crashed to the floor. Hot, brown liquid sloshed everywhere. I swiped the napkins off my tray and bent down to swab up the mess. All the café patrons turned at the commotion I'd caused, but I couldn't pry my gaze from one in particular. His head swiveled around—brown eyes, olive skin, and most definitely *not* Caleb. Disappointment burned though me like acid poured on a gaping wound.

"I'm so sorry." My voice quaked with emotion as I handed the customer some extra napkins for the splatter that found its way onto his lap. "I'll clean this up and get you a fresh cup."

Sophia met me at the counter and snatched the tray full of soiled napkins from my hands. "Melissa will take care of this. Go on a break." She jerked her head in the direction of the back room.

"Yeah, because Melissa isn't doing anything," Melissa grumbled and deposited the dishes she'd just cleared from two tables in the sink. She paused to wipe the sweat from her mocha brow with the back of her hand then noticed Sophia's glare. Her shoulders slumped and she relented, "I'll get right on it."

"I'm fine," I lied and reached over the stack of dirty dishes to wash the coffee from my hands. They shook so severely I clasped them firmly together and turned my shoulder before Sophia noticed. "We're slammed today and can't afford to be shorthanded."

"Yes, we can. Take a break, Celeste. You need it. Besides, you've got company."

I turned and glanced out the glass front wall of the shop. Rowan cruised across the parking lot on Caleb's bike.

Sophia's crimson lips pursed. "Did you call him?"

"No." I shook my head and shifted my gaze away to hide my guilt.

"Then it's just a coincidence that the one guy on the planet that can ease those bothersome feelings you're having just *happened* to pick this precise moment to bring that motorcycle back to you?"

I fiddled with my ring, flipping the emerald framed diamond around on my finger. "He had to bring it back to me. The timing is just … lucky."

Sophia's eyes narrowed. "You know, sometimes when two mystical beings are tuned in to each other they can begin to pick up on each other's feelings without even trying. It's rare, but I've seen it happen between kindred spirits."

"Hah! We're far from kindred spirits." I felt the weight of her stare drilling into my back even as I busied myself throwing ingredients into the blender. "We're just two people helping each other through a difficult time."

She stepped in close enough to whisper in my ear, "I know that's what it started as, but are you sure that's what it still is? Maybe things have changed for him? You're an empathe, there's a very easy way to find out … "

I hit blend to drown her out. When the machine finished I poured the foam beverage in a to-go cup and snapped on a lid. "I don't need to use my ability, because there's nothing there. The guy can barely tolerate me, he just feels the need to help me because of the bond he had with Caleb. We're performing a service for each other. That's it. Plus, he's as untrustworthy as they come. He'd stab me in the back in a heartbeat if there were something in it for him. Honestly, I wouldn't even go so far as to call him my friend."

"Oh, yeah?" One scarlet painted nail jabbed in the direction of my hand. "You give free Vanilla Bean Frappucinos with extra whip cream to all your non-friends?"

I glanced from the cup to her and back again. "Oh, shut up."

Ω ✳ ⅏

Sometimes muttering like a crazy person is mandatory and this was one of those times. "She doesn't know what she's talking about. We're two people helping each other cope. That's it. Sure, he doesn't ask me to give it back to him as much as he used to, but that's because he has a heart the size of a pea that emotions in general are foreign to. Not because of any new, weird, *incredibly inappropriate*, and insanely unwanted feelings that have developed on his part."

I shielded my eyes from the bright afternoon sun and peered around the parking area. I spotted him at the far end of the lot, leaning against the bike with his arms crossed over his chest. The short sleeves of his black t-shirt slid up to display all but the shoulders of his bronzed, muscular arms. His face was tipped toward the sun. The light made his hair glow like a golden halo. With a casual indifference his head lulled my way. There was no denying the guy was hot. That didn't change the fact that he was a self-centered ass.

Still ... my mind wandered as I walked over. Did he seem happy to see me? Anxious for me to get to him? I toyed with the idea of opening myself up to his emotions but quickly decided against it. Whatever he felt for me—good, bad, or indifferent—I really didn't want to know. It could ruin our arrangement and that was all that was holding me together as of late. For the sake of my mental well being I decided to take Rowan's cool detachment at face value.

He held out my keys and reached for the Frappucino. "Trade ya?"

As soon as his hand closed around the cup, I snatched mine away. We couldn't have any lingering touches that might add credibility to Sophia's claims.

Rowan's flaxen brows lowered and one side of his mouth pulled back in amusement. "Much appreciation for the drink, lass."

I shoved the keys into the pocket of my khaki work pants. "Okay look, I accept that you were a pirate a few centuries ago, but I'm not buying the lingo. Truth be told I think you force it."

He cocked his head to the side and peered at me from behind his sunglasses. "Well, aren't you a treat today. I'm inclined not to share my little gift if you're going to be nasty."

Panic churned my stomach at the idea of going the rest of the day without a moment's relief. "Sorry," I murmured and scuffed my tennis shoe against the pavement. "Rough day."

"Then let's get this over with quickly." He took a quick swig of his drink and wiped his mouth on the back of his hand. "Before you feel the need to tell me about it."

I shot him a glare that he ignored as he reached out and caught my hand.

"*What are you doing?*" Mild hysteria morphed my voice into a high-pitched squawk and I ripped my hand out of his grasp.

His eyebrows nearly shot off his head. He kept his voice low and even as he tried to break through my fog of crazy. "You remember how this works, yes? I *have* to touch you if you want me to work my magic. Or, you can continue to act like a loon, in which case I'll scamper meself off and leave you to that."

"You grabbed my hand. There's … meaning behind that." My cheeks and ears burned bright red. "I just don't want anything to be misconstrued here."

A wry smirk curled its way across his lips. "That's what you're worried about? What other people think?" Before I could answer he smacked his hand down on my face. His palm mashed my nose to the side. "What about this? Could this be misconstrued in anyway?"

"I hate you," I muttered from behind his hand.

"Yeah, I'm not your biggest fan either," he grumbled.

Rowan kept his hand plastered to my face as he gave me the emotional sedation I needed. My frayed nerves calmed and the pain lessened—for the moment. I exhaled a relieved, cleansing breath.

Rowan didn't linger. Quick and unceremoniously he yanked his hand off my face like a suction cup. "I'm sure I'll be seeing ya tonight, *Mo Chroi.*"

He vanished in a cloud of smoke.

Sophia was obviously wrong. Rowan didn't see me as his kindred spirit. All I was to him was a burden to bear and that was okay by me.

CHAPTER FIFTEEN

Bing.

"Attention Airscape travelers; there has been a gate change. Flight 183 departing to Orlando is now at Gate 45. Thank you."

Her banner rustled and Alaina dropped it below her chin. "What did that say? Was that her flight? I wasn't listening. Do we need to move? If so we should hurry!" She was so excited if she were a puppy she would've already piddled on the floor.

Kendall smoothed her hand over Alaina's long auburn waves. "That wasn't us. We're right where we need to be. Breathe, Lani."

"Oh! Good!" Up went the banner. "Let me know when she gets off the plane. I can't see anything back here."

I couldn't help but stare. "Alaina, isn't all this ... " I waved my arm at the spectacle that was Alaina, " ... a bit much?"

A corner of the banner curled out. Moss green eyes peeked out at me. "Absolutely not! I've never met my future mother-in-law before! I want her to recognize me as the bride and—more importantly—I want her to like me!"

"Well, first of all," I clasped my hands together and pressed them to my lips, "there are four people picking her up from the airport. One is her betrothed son. Two are her daughters. I'm fairly certain my mother is clever enough to figure out that the girl here she *didn't* give birth to is the bride. But perhaps you could explain to me how the veil, bride-to-be t-shirt, and gigantic sparkly 'O'Brien-Garrett Wedding or Bust' sign are supposed to make her like you?"

Alaina lowered the sign once more. It thumped to the ground under the weight of all that glitter and left a sparkly pile on the floor. "Because, I want her to think I'm a normal girl up-to-date on all the current nuptial traditions and customs, and *not* a three century old ex-Spirit Guide that has no place marrying her son."

"I think it's safe to say that won't be the first conclusion she comes to," I chuckled and checked the time on my phone. Her plane would land any minute now.

"I think her get up was a great idea," Gabe added through a giant mouthful. "Got us free *Cinnabons*!"

"Ah, yes. The true reason to announce your impending nuptials publicly every chance you get—to get free crap."

Gabe nudged me with his big, meaty shoulder. "Come on, Cee. You know if it was your wedding you'd be embracing all the goofy, fun traditions, too."

Kendall sucked in a shocked breath. Alaina's hand fluttered up to her mouth. Gabe seemed unaffected and took another huge bite of *Cinnabon*. The ring Caleb gave me seemed to burn its painful reminder against my skin.

Not wanting to ruin this moment for Alaina, I swallowed my emotions and forced on a big, jovial grin. "Well, I'm not! So no worries there!" Even I winced at the insane shriek that came out of my mouth. I cleared my throat and attempted to sound normal. "Hey, look, Mom's flight status just changed to arrived."

Gabe brushed the crumbs of his hands on his khaki shorts and nodded in the direction of the escalators. "I think this is her flight coming down now."

Alaina bounced on the balls of her feet, as her excitement reached a boiling point. She held her poster board high and shook it side to side. Rainbow glitter rained down.

Kendall spotted her first and waved her arm to catch Mom's eye. "There she is! Mom!"

A smile spread across my face. I had no idea just how much I'd missed her until that very moment. Her warm grin beamed down at us as she waved back and stepped onto the escalator. Keni looked like a carbon copy of our Mom. Same blue eyes, same delicate features, same porcelain skin, and same slender dancer physiques. The only difference—other than age—was that Mom kept her platinum locks in a chin-length bob.

She reached the bottom of the escalator and hurried to us with open arms. The black carry-on bag slung over her shoulder bobbed against her hip. "My babies!"

Keni rushed to meet her. Mom's arms locked around her in a firm hug. She pulled back and took Keni's face in her hands. "I've missed that face. You're letting your hair grow back out!" Kendall shook her head to allow Mom to see the full effect of her almost shoulder length 'do. "I like it! For the life of me I don't know why you hacked it off in the first place."

Mom turned to Gabe, which allowed Kendall a moment to shoot me a grimace. I answered with an understanding nod.

The truthful answer of, *"Well, Mother, I lost interest in my luxurious locks after a demon tangled his hand in it and utilized it to torture me,"* failed the appropriate airport conversation test.

"Gabe Allen, look at you!" Mom gave him a playful slap to his enormous chest before she wrapped her arms around him. "My little boy all grown up and getting married!" She peered up at him, her expression suddenly serious. "Don't tell anyone I'm old enough to have a married son or they're going to stop believing I'm twenty-seven."

"Your secret's safe with me." He grinned and bent his head to plant a kiss on her cheek. "It's good to see you, Mom. I'm really glad you came."

"I wouldn't have missed it for the world." Pride radiated from her smile.

I took a deep breath a second before her gaze settled on me. Would she sense a difference? Would my pain be apparent to her? Maybe the edge to my demeanor would be unmistakable?

"Celeste, my little Celeste." I nestled into her arms and inhaled her soft, flowery perfume. She plucked the nagging thought from my mind and whispered in my ear, "Your Grams told me you and that boy broke up. I'm sorry, honey."

She leaned back and used her index finger to tilt my chin up. Her gaze scoured my face, "You doing okay with it?"

My voice caught in my throat. Kid Celeste wanted to burst out in hysterical sobs and unload the whole sordid tale on her. To let her hold me, rock me, and murmur some wonderful Mommy words of wisdom designed to make everything all better. But I was a warrior now and had made the right decision. I couldn't let myself second-guess that. The savage looking version of myself I saw only in a dream refused to let those tears fall.

"Yeah, Mom, I am. It's hard, but I know it's for the best."

Mom pressed her palm gently to my cheek. "That's a very grown up way to look at it. It'll get easier, I promise."

Her arms slid away from me too soon. My inner child kicked my inner warrior in the shin for the missed opportunity.

Alaina whipped her sign in Kendall's direction and dove at our mother. The gaudy banner lashed across my sister's thighs and showered glitter all over her.

"Mom! Can I call you Mom? It's so great to meet you!" Alaina grasped our mother in a tight bear hug.

"And this must be Alaina?" Mom chuckled. "Could you loosen your grip just a little, sweetie? So I can see your pretty face … and maybe breathe?"

"Oh! Sorry!" Alaina retracted her death grip and clasped her hands behind her back. I smirked. Alaina's expression gave away her internal struggle to not latch on again like an overzealous koala bear.

Mom held her at arms distance—a wise idea—and cocked her head to the side to admire the bride to be. "Aren't you a vision? A regular blushing bride."

She glanced over her cardigan-clad shoulder at Gabe. "You did good, son. She looks like a keeper. "

Gabe grinned and shoved his hands in his pockets. "Yeah, she's all right." The indifference of his words held no weight against the love that emanated off of him as he gazed at his future bride.

I had that once. Only for a moment.

My heart constricted in a tight fist of pain. I bit down on the inside of my cheek hard enough to draw blood. I couldn't do this ... couldn't let myself fall apart and ruin things for Gabe and Alaina. It occurred to me that I might want to ask a certain blond pirate to be my date for the wedding. That way he could give me a much needed boost if the displays of love and affection left me curled up in the fetal position whimpering beside the aisle.

"So, tell me about yourself, Alaina. I want to know everything about the girl that won my boy's heart."

Not everything, I mused to myself.

"I'm twenty-three!" Alaina blurted a few octaves too loud. Mom winced in surprise. "Exactly twenty-two months older than Gabe which is a perfectly acceptable and not at all unusual age difference!"

"That's true," Mom said slowly and looked to me with confusion.

I smiled back in a way I hoped she read as nope, nothing out of the ordinary going on here.

Gabe wrapped an arm around his petite—and now visibly sweating—redhead to point her in the direction of baggage claim. "How about if we get Mom's bags and get her home? She needs to get settled in before all the festivities begin, right?"

A wide-eyed Alaina nodded, but kept her lips pressed together in a tight line. I recognized the look of someone holding their crazy in. I wore it often myself.

Mom hooked arms with Kendall and me as we trailed the happy couple out.

"She seems ... sweet," Mom stated diplomatically.

"She is, Mom," I confirmed. "She's just nervous about meeting you."

"There's no time for nerves! Lots to do!" She raised her shoulders when she grinned, a gesture that made her look more like a teenager than a mom. "So, what's first on the agenda?"

Wedding Planner Kendall fielded that question. She plucked her phone from her purse and tapped open her schedule. "Alaina's final dress fitting is tonight. Celeste and I can also pick up our dresses and make sure they don't need any further alterations. Tonight the football team is picking Gabe up at nine for a special Bachelor Party they planned for him. Tomorrow is spa day for us girls followed by decorating the hall."

Mom and Keni squealed and giggled their excitement.

I cringed. "What time is the fitting?"

"Five," Keni chirped with a toss of her hair.

I glanced down at my phone. If I timed it right I could get an emotional pick me up from Rowan before embarking to the land of ruffles, satin, and lace.

CHAPTER SIXTEEN

I don't do pink. More than that, I don't do flowery. But there I stood in *both* of those things. I turned my head to one side and then the other. My reflection didn't lie. I looked like a big pink shower loofah. The fuchsia, A-lined dress stopped just above my knees. Satin fabric hugged my torso then exploded out in a wide, poofy skirt. Big, pink flowers lined the bottom of the dress. The matching choker made it look as though one of the flowers leapt off the dress and suctioned itself to my neck like a leech. Nothing about this ensemble was in any way flattering.

Then again, maybe I reflected my bad mood onto the dress. Rowan ignored all my attempts—of both modern communication means *and* beating on his apartment door like a ticked off orangutan—to get a hold of him. Without his emotional booster shot I was a walking, talking little grey rain cloud that could easily make the jump to raging storm with even the slightest provocation.

The dressing room curtain swooshed across its rod as Kendall slid it back and gasped. "Oh! You look so pretty!"

I rolled my eyes. "No, I don't. I look like I fought a Cotton Candy demon and lost. Yet this same dress looks sensational on you. How is that fair?"

She waved off my words with a flick of her hand. I noticed her nails were already the matching shade of pink. "You know what would *really* make this outfit though? My wings! How great would they look with this? I could even spray them with pink glitter!"

"Your wings are not a fashion accessory, Kendall."

"I know." She pouted. "Just sayin'…"

"Come on out girls! Let's have a look-see!" Grams called.

Vicki's Bridal served free champagne. Grams celebrated this discovery by polishing off a whole bottle by herself. She had since tried on every veil and loudly declared this her new favorite hangout. The bingo hall would be very disappointed.

Kendall led the way out of the dressing room area. She bounded out to where Grams and Mom sat and went up on point to twirl for them. Her dress fanned out around her. They oohed and aahed accordingly.

I shuffled out behind her and tried to blend into the rack of prom dresses. Mom took one look at me, grimaced and bit down on her lower lip.

Gram's face pinched in distaste. "You sure you're wearing that neck flower right, Celeste? Darn thing's as big as your head. Doesn't look like that on Kendall."

"Now, Gladys, I think she looks lovely." Mom knew me well enough to know if she didn't speak up I'd tear the flower off and mash it into the floor with the heel of my tennis shoe. "Celeste, why don't you go see if Alaina needs help getting into her dress?"

Sure Mom was patronizing me, but what did it matter? I looked like a tool. A second before I turned away I caught a glimpse of my grandmother's decorated leg. "Grams, why are you wearing six garters?"

Her leopard print muumuu slid up her thigh and she hoisted her leg in the air. "I'm trying to decide which one to get to wear for Dr. Allyn. I'm thinking the black and pink. Which do you like? Julia isn't being any help at all."

"No, Julia isn't." My mom picked up a dress magazine and flipped through it to drive that point home.

I decided to follow Mom's lead and avoid the question all together. "You're right, Mom. Alaina probably could use some help."

Kendall chimed in with an exuberant response. "I like the pink with purple ribbon, Grams. But you're right, the black and pink is more your style."

"Thank you, *Kendall*." Grams put her leg down and slid off the unwanted garters.

I paused beside my sister and whispered, "Way to go, sis. You just gave our seventy-two year old grandmother tips on what she should wear for naughty fun with her sixty-five year old boyfriend."

Her angelic face fell as the horror of that realization sunk in.

I patted her shoulder. "Yep, you earned that mental image. Enjoy!"

Halfway down the hall I paused when I heard Grams mutter, "Seriously, that girl's gonna walk down the aisle looking like her bouquet is attacking her."

I filled my lungs to capacity and exhaled slowly. "Weddings are so friggin' magical."

⋐ ✴ ⋑

Unlike the bridesmaids, who were shoved in a closet with a sheet for a door, the brides at Vicki's Bridal got an entire room to themselves to shimmy into their gowns. I rapped softly on the six-panel door.

Alaina's voice filtered through softly, "Come in."

I grasped the polished brass handle and pushed open the door. Like a delicate swan, she turned her head in my direction. Her auburn waves were pinned back in an elegant twist to reveal the bare porcelain skin of her neck and shoulders. The beaded strapless bodice molded to her. At her hips the dress belled out in ruffle after ruffle of chiffon and taffeta. The traditional white dress got a splash of color from the fuchsia sash tied around her waist. On the side of it were three full, pink flowers.

Despite how stunning she looked, her forehead creased with concern. "What do you think? Will Gabe like it?"

I crossed to her and fastened the top two buttons she had missed. "How could he not? You look like a princess. *His* princess."

She peered back at her reflection and exhaled through pursed lips. Her hands smoothed the cascading waves of her skirt. "It's not at all like what the women wore on their wedding day during my time."

I got a pit in my stomach that Kendall may have forced her fashion sense. "But you like it, *right*?"

She nodded, but doubt swirled in her eyes. "I do. I really do. It's a gorgeous dress and fitting for *this* point in time. What I always envisioned myself getting married in wouldn't have."

I gave her shoulders a quick squeeze. "As long as you're sure you're happy with it. But honestly, you could walk down the aisle in Gabe's football jersey and he'd still think you were the most beautiful woman he'd ever seen."

"Actually, I think he'd prefer the jersey," Alaina giggled. The tension she'd been holding in her shoulders relaxed a little. "Would you please help me with my veil? For the life of me I can't figure out how to get it to stay on."

"Not sure I'm the right person for that job. Any fashion related issues are strictly Kendall territory. But I'll give it my best shot." I bent down and extracted the veil from its box on the floor. The thin tiara was a collage of tasteful crystal and pearl flowers with long sheer lace that trailed from the back. Just as I stood to fluff out the fabric, a loud, dragging, scratch shook the wall behind me. The hair on the back of my neck tried to stand on end but a flower the size of a dinner plate weighed it down.

My head whipped in Alaina's direction. "Did you hear that?"

"Maybe it was a mouse?"

The noise came again, this time more pronounced and deliberate. It began at the top of the wall by the mirror and drew down to the floor with enough force to knock bits of plaster free.

"That's no mouse." I grabbed Alaina by the shoulders and shoved her toward the door. "Get my mom and Grams out of here *now,* and tell Keni I'm gonna need her."

The ominous dragging began again. A chunk of drywall gave way and something black and shiny jutted through, and then quickly disappeared back into the wall.

Alaina squealed and slapped both hands over her mouth. "How do I get your mother out of here without alarming her?"

I kept my tone calm and assertive. "Alaina, you're the bride. What you say goes. If you go out there and tell them you forgot your special wedding bra and can't possibly get an accurate fitting without it, they'll jump to get it for you. Now pull it together and *go!*"

She gathered up her billowing skirt and bolted down the hall.

I heard the awed gasps of my mother and Grams when Alaina made her entrance. Then two beats later the doorbell at the front of the store chimed. Alaina had accomplished her objective.

The noisemaker apparently gained a partner—or three. The foreboding drag now emanated from four different spots on the wall.

Kendall sauntered into the room, shut the door behind her, and with a roll of her shoulders released her wings. "See? Told ya this dress would look fab with them."

"Not really the time, Keni." I jerked my head at the crumbling wall.

"What is it?"

"No idea."

As suddenly as the noise began, it stopped. Movement of any kind ceased. We had fought enough demons to know that nothing good ever follows a silence like this. Kendall arched her wings up high behind her. I brought my arms up and balled my hands into fists, just as the wall in front of us exploded with enough force to shake the ground under our feet. Kendall pivoted and shielded us both from the shower of plaster chunks that assaulted the room. A spider so big its back grazed the ceiling emerged from the blown out wall covered in a white haze of drywall dust.

"No! No way! I wasn't crazy about the dragon, but I draw the line at spiders! There has to be a no arachnids clause somewhere in our calling!"

"Oh, there's claws all right," I added, only half listening to her. The long, black legs of the creature stretched out toward us. We pressed our backs up against the wall behind us and began to inch our way to the door. "But I'm more concerned about the mandibles. Look at the size of those things!"

Kendall reached the door first. Her hand circled my wrist. In a blur of wind and speed she flew us out of the dressing room and down the hall where we collided with Alaina. The three of us rolled to the ground in a mass of satin, tulle, and feathers.

"Why are you still here?!" I shrieked and tried to kick myself free from Alaina's train.

"I wanted to make sure you were oka-*aahhhhh*!" Alaina's words morphed into a scream when the spider came into view. Its legs clicked across the wall as it skittered sideways straight toward us.

"Is everything okay? I heard screams." Vicki, the plump, southern bell storeowner rounded the corner, took one look at the spider and passed out cold.

"Fan-friggin-tastic! Alaina, get her out of here!" Finally free of the mass of fabric, I jumped up and looked around for a weapon. "Where's a giant rolled up newspaper when you need one?"

Alaina scrambled to her feet, hooked Vicki under her arms, and dragged her through the door that led to the front of the store. The spider eased its way off the wall and onto the floor. Its claws pinched and snapped at the air. Goo dripped from mandibles that chomped hungrily.

Beside me Keni gulped. "Please tell me you have a plan."

"That depends." Fear raised the decibel of my voice to a squeak. If that thing lunged there was a good chance I was gonna let loose a girlie scream that went completely against the superhero image. "Do you consider running a plan? 'Cause that's all I've got."

"Absolutely!"

We both spun on our heels and sprinted for the showroom. The spider gave chase. I grabbed a rack of prom dresses and knocked it to the ground to slow down the monstrous insect. The spider hissed and easily stepped over the brightly colored pile of sequins and ruffles.

Something whizzed by my head. A zebra print pump slammed into one of the spider's six eyes and the creature reared back in pain.

"Good thinking, Keni!" I shouted and joined her at the shoe display.

I palmed a sequined stiletto with an exceptionally pointy heel and launched it as hard as I could. It embedded in the spider's head. The creature stumbled to the side and smashed into the glass display case of tiaras and jewelry. Glass shattered. Expensive jewelry crunched under its pedipalp.

Unfortunately, the blows injured it but neither incapacitated nor killed. The spider raised one back leg and knocked the stuck shoe free. Then it charged. Eight legs clicked across the wood floor in rapid-fire succession toward me. I whipped any object within reach at it. Shoes. Purses. Veils. Hangers. Dresses. Crinoline. Kendall joined in and together we made it rain formal wear on the giant insect. None of it slowed the big bug down at all, but it sure looked pretty.

From behind me came the hiss of metal being unsheathed. I risked a glance over my shoulder and found myself staring into a pair of brown eyes caked heavily with Goth make-up. A curtain of ink black hair framed her ghostly white complexion. I didn't have to look down to know she'd be clad in skank wear.

"Kat," I spat at Alec's little toy. He'd taken a normal college girl and demonfied her into a plaything for himself. Between her and the spider this didn't bode well.

Her black painted lips curled up in a snide grin. "Conduit."

The spider picked that moment to lunge. Its pincher slashed Kendall's upper arm, tearing open her flesh. As she shrieked in pain, I grabbed her good arm and yanked her behind me. Kat shoving me out of the way and meeting the bug head on interrupted any further heroics I had planned. She swung the metal barb that extended from her wrist and hacked off one of the spider's pinchers. Black blood sprayed across the room. The angry arachnid reared up and swiped its remaining claw at Kat's bare midsection. (Seriously, who wears a tube top to a demon fight?)

Kendall closed her wing around her arm and a soft glow radiated off of her as she healed the vicious looking wound. Now that I knew she was safe, I turned to throw myself into the mix, but only made it two steps before a strong, bear-sized hand closed around my upper arm.

"I wouldn't do that if I were you," a deep voice rumbled. "Kat gets cranky if she doesn't get to fight solo." I gaped up at the easily seven-foot tall, building of a man. His skin was black as night, his smile blindingly white.

Keni's pink and purple shadowed eyes widened. "Hey, aren't you Trent Cummings, the NFL player that went missing like a month ago? Dude you are, like, all over *E!*."

"That's who I used to be." Trent rounded his neck and arched his back. Metal spikes shot out of his spine and down the backs of his arms. "I got a new life now."

I still wanted in on the fight despite the presumed dead football player's warning. This was *my* calling dang it! I didn't need the Goth Skank Queen's help! I spun back just as Kat latched on to the remaining pincher and used it to swing herself on to the spider's back. She straddled it like a horse and buried her barb deep into its head. The spider's legs splayed out to the sides as its massive body crumpled to the ground and dissolved into black ooze. All the sparkly, frilly accessories and dresses on the ground got doused with a layer of dead demonic spider sludge.

Kat landed gracefully on her feet and retracted her barb. She looked me up and down with blatant contempt. "Alec sends his love. He says he'll be seeing you soon. Oh, and nice neck flower." She snorted a mocking laugh then disappeared in a cloud of smoke before I could make a witty reply.

How rude was that?

"That's my cue," Trent murmured in his deep tremor and copied Kat's exit strategy.

Kendall and I stood in silence and surveyed the destroyed bridal shop. Black slime dripped from every surface and streaked down the walls. All the beautiful formal wear Vicki displayed in her showroom was a total loss. My guilt got the best of me and I tried to rectify the situation a little by righting one of the display racks. It bumped the wall and caused a giant glop of spider sludge to drip from the ceiling and plop down right on my head. Black ooze slowly seeped through my hair and trickled down my face.

Kendall dry heaved beside me. "Oh that's beyond nasty! I'm gonna puke just looking at you!"

The life of a superhero. Glamorous, no?

CHAPTER SEVENTEEN

Silk webbing tied my hands to my sides. My attempts to wiggle them loose only bound me tighter. A shadow fell over me. Dreading what I would see I was slow to lift my head. Coarse, wiry hair surrounded six solid black eyes. The spider's mandibles twitched in anticipation. I opened my mouth to scream, but it sprayed webbing that gagged me to silence. Tears of terror streamed down my face as the gigantic insect lowered its head …

"Celeste? Get up." Keni shook me awake.

I tried to sit up, but something had my limbs knitted in tight. Fearing it was spider webbing, I kicked and flailed for all I was worth. "What the heck?! Get it off! *It's on me!*"

Finally, I freed myself from the reality of a constricting bed sheet by falling off the bed in a heap of covers. I sat there panting, trying to steady my blood pressure.

Kendall peered down at me, her dramatically made up eyes widened in surprised confusion. "Smooth there, Chosen One."

"Bad dream," I murmured then wadded up my comforter and tossed it back on my bed.

One side of Keni's hot pink glossed mouth pulled back in a wry smirk. "Well, it's over now and you need to get dressed. We've got *big* plans. Put this on." She threw a black article of clothing at me that smacked me in the face before falling into my lap.

I stumbled to my feet and stretched up on my toes with arms arched up over my head as I tried to release sleep's heavy hold on me. Maybe it was the awful dreams about being eaten alive but I didn't feel rested in the least. Not that I could admit to that. Today was Spa Day and any lack of enthusiasm on my part would *not* be well received. As obsessive as Kendall had been about planning this, if I didn't strap on my best fake smile she might have me voted out of the family.

I pulled off my jammie top and exchanged it for the one my sister insisted I wear. I slid it over my head then found myself lost in rows of strappy black fabric. With my arms still in the air and a mess of material clinging to me, I struggled to find arm or head holes. The correlations between this and the spider web dream that was still fresh in my mind had me teetering on the edge of a hissy fit.

"Kendall!" My voice came out high and frantic. "What the crap is wrong with this shirt? Fix it or I'm gonna rip it to shreds to get it off!"

Keni heaved an annoyed sigh at the burden she suffered of having a fashion illiterate sister. She turned me toward the full-length mirror on the back of our closet door. With a pull here and a tug there the shirt fell right into place. Okay, "shirt" seems a somewhat liberal description for what now covered my torso. Suspended from each of my shoulders was a thick strap of black fabric. From those straps hung a mesh of thinner straps that covered my arms, chest, and stomach. The material covered what needed covering, but a whole lot of skin still showed through. A fact I was not at all comfortable with.

"Uh, Keni? Exactly what kind of spa is this?"

"It's midnight, Cee. We're not going to the spa. I've got other plans for us." Kendall's eyes glittered mischievously beneath a thick layer of eyeliner.

My forehead creased when I finally noticed what my sister was wearing; a one-sleeved black tank top covered in sequins, short pink mini-skirt, fishnet stockings, and knee high black boots.

Her hair had been twisted, pinned, and sprayed to stick up off her head in a purposefully messy 'do. A pink scarf was knotted around her upper arm.

"And these plans involve dressing like we're in a Ke$ha video?"

She crossed to my dresser, yanked out a pair of jeans, and threw them at me. "The spa day just sounded, like, totally dull. So I canceled it. Instead we're gonna have some *real* fun."

"It sounded *dull*?" I kicked off the guys boxers I'd wore to bed and wiggled into my jeans. "*You* planned it! You've been rambling on about it since Gabe put that stupid rock on Alaina's finger!"

She raised her eyebrows and gave me that "chill out, you freak" look all teenage girls perfect. "So I changed my mind. It happens. Get over it. *Geesh.*"

If this was some lingering after effect from her break-up with Keith, I sincerely hoped she got over it quick. I could only bite my tongue for so long before I'd run out of nice. For now, I decided to let her 'tude slide—especially since I wasn't crazy about a spa day anyway. I zipped up my jeans and shook the legs straight. "So what are we doing instead?"

She hooked her arm around mine and steered me over to our desk. Placing her hands on my shoulders, she shoved me down in the chair. The sight of her tackle box full of makeup and hair accessories opened and at the ready scared me almost as much as my nightmare.

"Oh, you'll see ... " she smirked.

03 ✳ 80

"I'm just saying, if my eyelids are heavy from the glitter there may in fact be *too* much glitter." My hair had been parted down the middle and pulled up in two pigtail knots. Add that to the mountain of makeup Kendall had slapped on me and the result was me looking like a clown hooker. I sincerely hoped

105

whatever plans Keni made didn't involve other visually capable human beings. I held fast to the handrail and struggled to maneuver the stairs in heels a good three inches higher than my comfort zone.

Kendall shoved past me and nearly sent me tumbling. "There's no such thing as too much glitter, now hurry up."

I cursed under my breath and shuffled my way to the bottom of the stairs. Across the foyer I teetered my way to the coat rack. In spite of the warm night, I wanted the cover my hoodie offered before I stepped foot out of the house.

"Oh, you don't need that!" Grams proclaimed as she bee lined it from the kitchen to the living room with a tray in her hands. She had donned her short, black party dress and leopard print pumps for our mystery occasion. I suddenly had a very bad feeling about this. Curiosity led me to the living room.

"Uh … where's all the furniture?" I gaped.

Everything had been emptied out of the room except for the coffee table that was pushed up against the back wall where Grams now set her tray. In the place of the rest of Grams' modern décor sat five folding chairs. Alaina waited in one, her legs crossed at the ankle and hands folded demurely in her lap.

Judging by her blush pink dress with its conservative neckline and pretty embroidered flowers she hadn't received the skank wear memo. "Gabe and the football team moved it all into the den at Grams request, right before they headed out to that owl themed restaurant."

"Owl themed?"

Her auburn locks danced when she nodded. "Yes, they have owls on all their signs and the waitress' shirts. While I've never been inside I assume men like the wilderness type atmosphere offered."

"Yeah, *that's* what the draw of that place is," I lied and snagged Keni from her task of running an extension cord from a side outlet to the center of the room. "The furniture is gone, there are red lights in the ceiling fixtures, and Grams just pulled a stack of singles out of her bra. Kendall, *please* tell me you didn't do what I think you did."

Kendall tried, and failed, to adopt an expression of mock innocence. "Why, Celeste, whatever do you think I did?"

"*What is the matter with you?* Our mother is here!" I hissed through clenched teeth. "You are sixteen! What do you think she's gonna say when ... "

"Oh, Celeste! There you are!" Mom sauntered up behind me and gave my arm a squeeze. "Isn't this exciting? Kendall arranged some sort of performance for us! I can't wait to see what it is! I love live theater!"

I waited until Mom sat in a chair by Alaina before I spun back on Kendall. "You know she's gonna kill *me* for this, right? You being young and impressionable, and all. "

"Probably." She nodded as if she had considered the likelihood of that very thing, but failed to see how it involved her. "So you might as well enjoy the show." The doorbell chimed and her face brightened. "I wonder who that could be? Alaina, why don't you go get the door?"

Alaina rose with a smile to do just that. I rushed to corner Grams. "You know this is going to end badly, right?"

"Yep, but it'll be fun!"

It seemed there was no stopping the inevitable. Since I sure as heck couldn't beat them—though I'd like to—I decided I might as well join them. I glanced down at the little glasses of green *Jell-O* Grams unloaded from her tray and decided that would be as good a place to start as any.

"Mmm ... desserts." I scooped one up and slurped it down.

"Celeste, no!" Grams said about five second too late.

"What *is* that, turpentine?" I cringed as it burned its way down my gullet.

Grams cast a guilty glance at my mom and muttered under her breath. "*Jell-O* shots. Don't have any more and don't tell your mother about that one."

I was still trying to shake off the grimace caused by *Jell-O a' la Grams* when a flustered-looking Alaina appeared in the doorway and waved her arm frantically to get my attention.

And so it begins. I stifled a groan and made my way over to her.

"The local law enforcement is here, an Officer Python?"

"Oh, that's classy," I snorted.

She talked right over me. Her voice shook with nerves. "He asked where he should set up. I'm not familiar with this tradition. What's happening?"

I made eye contact with Kendall and jerked my head toward the foyer, and then I laid a comforting hand on Alaina's shoulder. "This is a somewhat new tradition in which the friends and loved ones of the bride-to-be go out of their way to mortify her."

Alaina's milky white skin went ashen.

"But don't worry, I'll be right there with you to help you through it, okay?" I hoped she didn't notice that the sour apple battery acid Grams allowed me to drink was already causing my words to come out slightly slurred.

"Everyone take your seats!" Kendall ordered. "It's showtime!"

As soon as we were seated the music was cued up. At the first few strums of *Black Betty* Alaina shot me a nervous glance. I gave her my best reassuring smile and a big thumbs up. Around the arched doorframe swung Officer Python. His fake cop shirt barely contained the rippling muscles beneath. A pair of mirrored glasses hid his eyes. His hat sat low on his forehead. It shielded his face and gave him an air of mystery normally hard to accomplish by someone wearing tear away pants.

Keni *woohoo*ed. Grams let out a loud catcall. Mom finally figured out what was happening, groaned and averted her eyes.

As the opening cords of the music thumped Officer Python—*geesh*—sashayed straight for Alaina. He wrapped his bulging arms around her, grabbed the sides of her chair, and dragged her to the center of the room. Alaina squealed and white knuckled her seat. My mom tossed back a *Jell-O* shot and glared at me. I ricocheted that same look to Kendall. She ignored me and carried on clapping her hands over her head.

Right in the blushing bride's face the "officer" wiggled his hips in time to the music. Alaina glanced awkwardly around the room, trying to figure out a safe place to look as the good officer tore open his shirt.

"Officer! Your shirt!" Alaina squeaked. "I don't believe this is protocol!"

Unfortunately for her he wasn't listening. He was too busy running his hands over his greased up abs and moving his hips to the rhythm. Grams leapt out of her chair and waved her wad of dollar bills. In one fluid motion, our gyrating "law enforcement" grabbed a fistful of material from his black slacks in each hand and ripped those babies clear off.

"Seems Velcro pants would be incredibly inconvenient when pursuing a suspect," Alaina's voice rose an octave with each word. She hid her face behind her hands and peeked through her fingers.

Clad in a snakeskin Speedo, Officer Python shimmied for all he was worth right in Alaina's face.

That was her breaking point. "Celeste!" she shrieked. "I'm scared! Am I under attack?! *Do I slap it?!*"

"Alrighty, that's enough." I rose from my chair, took a moment to let the world stop spinning, and went to my future sister-in-law's aid. I walked up behind our hardworking entertainer and rested an arm on each greased up bicep. "You're doing a great job. Really. Top notch." I shuffled him a few steps over and turned him in Grams direction. "But maybe you could just point that … here."

He never missed a beat, as he switched to a much more receptive audience. Behind Grams I saw Mom clap her a hand over Kendall's eyes. Served her right. She lost her mind when she got the bright idea to plan this. Now she didn't even get to watch. *Ha-ha*.

Stripper fiasco behind us, I offered a hand to Alaina. Without a word exchanged we headed straight for the coffee table where we both helped ourselves to a serving of j-e-l-l-o. She was over three hundred, well within legal age. I'm the Chosen One and warrior of the world so I earned one, too. Of course, I turned my back to my mommy in case she disagreed.

Bernard just *had* to pick that moment to poof in by the door. "Conduit!"

My mother's blue eyes bulged and she nearly fell off her chair. "What the heck is in that *Jell-O*? I'm seeing talking lawn ornaments!"

"Well that's just offensive." Bernard crossed his arms and huffed.

I jerked my head in the direction of the other room. Bernard got the message and scurried his little legs out as quickly as they could carry him. Duty bound and more than a little tipsy, I followed.

I didn't realize Alaina trailed me until Bernard scowled in her direction. "There's no need for her to be here. She's no longer a Guide."

Alaina flinched as if Bernard had slapped her. Despite how thrilled she was for her upcoming wedding I knew she still missed her supernatural role and the powers that went along with them. She took a step back in retreat, but I grabbed her wrist and pulled her back by my side.

"But she *is* family." I peered down at Bernard and blinked hard. For a second there I saw three of him; which was a terrifying image. "Plus, if she goes back in there she'll be traumatized further by a snake-skinned banana-hammock and I can't subject her to that."

Bernard's eyes narrowed. He waved his cane and floated up to my eye level. He leaned in close and sniffed my breath. His face instantly set in a frown of disapproval. "You're drunk!"

"I am not!" Bad time for a hiccup-burp that reeked of alcohol.

Bernard wrinkled his nose and waved the smell away with one stubby little hand. He floated back down and stamped his cane against the hardwood floor. "You are the Chosen One! You have to be ready to fight at a moment's notice! This is unacceptable. I thought your cavalier attitude toward your calling had improved, but clearly I was mistaken."

"It was a one-time accidental thing!" I slurred, and then leaned one hand up against the wall. The room suddenly seemed slanted. *Weird.* "And it's not like I planned this. I was in bed dreaming of terrifying giant bugs and Kendall forced me out of bed to watch a half-naked man wiggle."

That mental image prompted a *teehee* from Alaina. Her reaction made me laugh and snort in a most un-feminine way, which sent us both into an uncontrollable giggling fit.

Bernard jabbed his cane in my direction. My laughter died a sudden death. I knew all too well what that stupid little stick could do. "Look at you! You're a mess! You couldn't spot a demon right now if it walked right up and ripped your nose off."

I held up one finger and tried my best to look indignant as I swayed side to side. "Okay A) I would *totally* notice that. 2) You have no room to talk, you and your little satchel of berries." Bernard's mouth fell open in haughty shock. *Jell-O* nerves encouraged me to press on. "That's right, I know about that! And D) I'm the Conduit." I spread my arms out wide, as if that provided explanation enough. My argument became less convincing when I had to latch onto Alaina to stop myself from toppling over. "It's in my blood to find and kill demons. No matter what kind of state I'm in I'm still a lean, mean, demon locating machine!"

"Celeste!" Kendall screamed. "The stripper's a demon! *Stripper's a demon!*"

Bernard folded his arms. He said nothing, but gave me an easy to decipher told ya so look.

"I had my suspicions," I lied. "Nobody's abs are *that* perfect."

CHAPTER EIGHTEEN

Alaina and I leaned back and peeked into the living room. Everything appeared normal. Music blared and Mom was dancing with the stripper under obnoxious red lights while Kendall and Grams watched. Okay … maybe *normal* isn't the right word. Disturbing, yet on par for the evening, seems more fitting.

Alaina cocked her head to the side. "Uh, Celeste? What's wrong with your mother's face?"

I squinted and tried to focus through my *Jell-O* goggles. My mother's peaches and cream complexion had been drained chalk white, a bluish hue encircled her formerly rosy lips.

"Why's she staring at the stripper like that?" I vocalized the ponderings of my inner monologue.

"If I had to guess," Bernard leaned against his cane and rested one hand on top of the other, "I'd say it's because without the hindrance of his mirrored glasses your exotic dancing demon has the ability to hypnotize his prey and suck the life out of them using nothing more than the power of his stare."

I whipped my head around so fast I swayed on my feet … or maybe that was from the stupid sky-high heels Kendall had crammed on my feet. "He's killing her?!"

"And yet you're still standing here talking to me," Bernard pointed out, then pulled a handful of berries from his satchel and popped them into his mouth.

I kicked off my shoes and ran into the living room just as Grams linked her arms around my mother's waist and heaved her to the side. The hold of the demon's glare instantly broke and Mom went limp. Grams eased her to the floor as gently as possible. The demonic stripper emitted a snake-like hiss and tried to fix his gaze on another target—Kendall. She shook her wings free, spun around, and expanded them wide to protect all of us from his stare.

"Whenever you're ready to step in here, *Conduit*, by all means go ahead," Kendall snipped. Sure, she had a point, since I was standing there doing nothing. But still—*rude*.

I had the makings of an idea—inklings really—and that was about it. "On the count of three, duck." The way my voice rose at the end made it sound like more of a question than a statement. Which it kind of was.

Kendall jerked her head in a brief nod.

"One."

Now would be a good time to figure out what you're gonna do, I thought to myself.

"Two."

Seriously, I got nothin' here.

"Three!" Kendall ducked down and I leapt through the air. In a tuck position I managed two complete rotations before I landed hard right on my butt behind the demon. I scrambled to my feet as he spun on me.

Grams waved her hands over her head and screamed, "Don't look him in the eye and for Pete's sake don't trash the house!"

I heeded her warning—that lady can be downright scary if you don't—and decided to take the fight outside. I put my shoulder down and ran at him like I'd watched Gabe do on the football field more times than I could count. He expelled a breathless *huunnh* when my shoulder connected with his gut. I clung to him and tried to whisk him out of the house in a blur of superhuman speed. Tried. It would've gone smoother had I not plowed us into two different walls before I shouted at Alaina, "Open the friggin' door already!"

114

I deposited Stripper Demon in the driveway, then put some much needed distance between us to allow myself a second to regroup. With my hands on my knees I tried to breathe through the wave of nausea brought on by the laced *Jell-O* and super speed combo. The demon stripper needed no such break. His lips curled back in a malicious grin as he took a menacing step in my direction. It didn't seem to bother him in the least that he was still in his undies.

I held up one finger. "Hold on a sec. We'll do this, I'm just gonna need a minute first."

His yellow snake eyes blinked to the solid black of a Seeker. "Oh no." A forked tongue darted from his mouth. "We're going to do thisssssss right now. I'm gonna sssssssuck the life out of you and I'm going to enjoy it. Assss the Chosen One I bet your esssssssence will be *delicioussssss.*"

"I get that you've got your demonic reputation to think of." His stride was more slither than walk as he inched my way. "But from one civilized person to another, I'm asking you to give me a minute here."

"A minute isssss all you have left." With a snake-like roll of his neck, he tried to catch my gaze.

My inability to focus suddenly felt like an asset as he failed to capture my gaze. "As menacing as a deadly staring contest is, I'm asking you to reconsider. Just take a brief pause. Then we'll engage in an epic battle that generations to come will marvel at. What do you say?"

"I sssssssay it'sssssss time to die, girl."

"Have it your way." I shrugged and raised my palm toward the neighbor's John Deer riding mower. I lifted it off the ground with a telekinetic boost, guided it through the air, and dropped it on the head of the pants-less demon. By the time its wheels bounced to the ground he disintegrated to black ooze.

"Oh yeah, the force is strong with me." I giggle-hiccuped.

"Given up entirely on attempts to be discreet, have we?" a husky voice murmured against my ear.

I spun around. Hands raised, palms out, to do ... something. Any attempt at intimidation disappeared when I tripped over my own feet and fell into my "attacker". Cradled in a pair of muscular arms, I peered up at a golden-haired hottie.

"Rowan!" I exclaimed loud enough to wake the sleeping neighborhood. "What're you doing here?"

"When ya didn't beat down me door tonight I worried some nasty demon had bested ya." He lifted his chin toward the lawn mower and demon goo. "Didn't realize the attire for your battles had become so lax."

"We were having a bachelorette party for Alaina, then the entertainment turned out to be—" I pushed off his chest, looked side-to-side to see for eavesdroppers, then cupped my hands around my lips and mouthed the word, "—evil."

"You're drunk."

"I am not!"

He raised one eyebrow and folded his arms over his chest.

"Okay, maybe a little," I tittered. A burp quickly turned that laugh to a grimace.

Disapproval oozed from every pore of him as he shook his head. "Fate of the world depends on your safety and you're standing out here in the middle of the night completely shnockered. Ya really don't have a lick of sense, do ya?"

"I have plenty of sense. *You're*," I poked my finger into his pec, "just a big grouch. You better start being nicer to me, or I won't ask you and your adorable chin dimple to go to my brother's wedding with me."

His stern exterior shattered and for reasons I didn't understand in the least he visibly struggled not to laugh. "You want me to be your date for the wedding? Even though—Heaven forbid—others might see?"

"Others-smothers!" I waved a dismissive hand in the air. "Just you, me, and this adorable little butt-chin. What do you say?" I punctuated my question by sticking my finger into his chin dimple and adding a, "Boop!"

Somewhere in the back of my mind a little voice whispered, "You'll regret this tomorrow." But that voice was *really* quiet and for some weird reason British.

Rowan grabbed my hand and held it away from his face. "As touching as this moment is, let's get you to bed to sleep it off before I answer."

I tried to plant my feet. An act I quickly found to be impossible with jelly legs. "No! Not until you agree to be my date."

He pressed his lips together. His gaze searched my face with an intensity that nearly caused another giggle fit. "Why are you asking me this? Is it *just* because of what I can do for you?"

Exhaustion quickly setting in and I let my head flop down on his shoulder. "Because you're the only one that knows what a big ole' mess I am. I don't have to pretend when I'm with yooo ... "

I passed out midsentence.

CHAPTER NINETEEN

I positioned the tulle to hide the white light-cord, then secured it with a thumbtack.

"It's uneven. Poofier on the right than the left."

I grumbled to myself and fluffed up the left side. "Tell me again why you're here?"

Rowan handed me a section of green ivy to drape over the tulle. "Right now I'd say I'm here to ensure that you don't make this freakishly large, yet incredibly fancy archway behind the bridal table, a travesty of oddly placed sparkle and frill that could ruin the bride and groom's special day."

From behind dark shades I shot him a glare he was sure to feel, even without me using my empathic skills. My head pounded from last night and I had no tolerance for him, bright lights, or loud noises.

He ignored my look and busied himself digging another vine of ivy out of the box. "No really, Gabe and Alana are wonderful people. Deserve all the happiness in the world and perfectly placed lights ... as it were."

"Alaina," I corrected and scooted my ladder over to the middle of the archway.

"Aye. Her, too."

Before I formed a suitable rebuttal, Alaina deterred the conversation as she buzzed up like a caffeinated humming bird. Her auburn hair was pulled back in a messy bun and her blouse hung lopsided from being buttoned wrong. Add that to her frantic gaze that darted here, there, and everywhere and it appeared our bride was on the verge of unraveling. "Celeste! Have you seen Kendall?"

I peered around the room, my forehead creased. "Actually, no. I haven't. Shouldn't she be here with a clipboard and a whip making sure every flower and candle is positioned exactly right?"

"Yes!" Alaina's hands came up like she wanted to grab someone and shake them. Rowan and I both jerked back ... just in case. "She has the centerpieces, the linens for the cake table, the guest book, *and* the wedding favors to go on the guest tables." She counted the items on her fingers before she jammed her pointer finger into her chest hard enough to make *me* wince. "Do you know what *I* have?"

Rowan and I exchanged looks.

"Does she expect us to answer?" he whispered out of the corner of his mouth.

A bit of her former eagle-self came out when she squawked, *"Do you?!"*

"Oh, she does."

"Terrified guests?" I slapped a hand over my mouth, surprised I'd let it slip out.

"No! I have three hundred guests attending my wedding *tomorrow* and no idea what's going on because your sister insisted on handling everything and then decided to vanish! What do I do, Celeste? *What do I do?*" Sweat dotted her brow as her chest rose and fell with each ragged breath.

I sidestepped the ladder, rounded the table, and took Alaina's hand. Centering myself, I found my personal calm. My well of inner strength tended to run dry frequently as of late, but I gave her all I still possessed. Peaceful essence flowed between us. "Kendall *will* be here. She will. In the meantime, you've got all your family and friends working to make sure everything will be beautiful."

The tension drained from her like someone pulled the plug on a full bathtub. Her breathing steadied and her hunched shoulders relaxed.

"Tomorrow you'll marry the man of your dreams and you'll get the happily ever after you've waited centuries for." I broke the link and dropped Alaina's hand before she felt my own sorrows sneaking in.

Alaina sighed. Once more she looked the part of the glowing bride-to-be. "Thank you. I needed that." Her emotional reprieve came not a moment too soon because the overly tanned caterer began shouting about some insufficient electrical outlet drama.

"Duty calls!" She grinned and trotted off, refreshed and regenerated.

Rowan sauntered up beside me and eased the tulle from my white-knuckled fist. To others it would appear a meaningless act, the simple exchange of fabric, but with that brief skin on skin contact he drowned my pain with hope and optimism. Then, wordlessly, he strode back over to the archway and climbed the ladder.

I stared after him, my mind blown by the realization that just occurred to me. "You knew today was going to be hard for me. That's why you came."

He raked his fingers through his hair and let his lips slide into a cocky leer. "As noble as that makes me sound, it's just not the case. My being here has less to do with your emotions and more to do with the startling revelations you made last night."

Heat rose in my cheeks. I quickly found a string of ivy that desperately needed untangling right that minute. "I don't know what you're talking about."

Rowan crossed his forearms on the top step and gave me a wink. "Perhaps you'd like to stick your finger in me chin dimple and refresh your memory?"

My face ignited with heat so intense it was surprising flames didn't shoot out my eye sockets. The voice in the back of my head put down its tea and crumpet long enough to mutter, *"See? I told you you'd regret it."*

I struggled to keep my expression neutral despite my radioactive glow. "Maybe decorating should be a silent activity."

છ✳ૹ

An hour later the second floor of the Gainesboro library— the town's *only* rentable hall space—bustled with pre-wedding activity. Gabe and his football players set up the guest tables under the watchful eye of the bride. Mom guided the florist through the space to show her where everything would be and what went where. Grams schooled the bartender on some of her homemade concoctions that I sincerely hoped he never tried on another human being.

I secured the last of the skirting to the bridal table and attempted to tune out Rowan's yammering. "I'm just sayin', *Mo Chroi*, ya begged me to be your date. Really. It was a deep yearning grovel that was most unbecoming."

"You planning on dropping this topic any time soon?" I muttered around the clip I held in my teeth.

He leaned over the table and wiggled his eyebrows suggestively. "The topic of how bad you want me? I'll drop it as soon as you admit ... "

In a flash I was on my feet, one hand held up to silence Rowan. He followed my stare to the intimidating large dude in black biker boots, faded jeans, dingy white tank top, and black leather vest that just entered. Imagine Dwayne "The Rock" Johnson minus the charismatic charm or basic approachability. Tattoos covered every visible inch of this guy's bulging arms and thick neck. He slid off his black shades and peered around the room with emotionless slate eyes. No doubt about it, this dude equaled bad news and he was dragging my little sister along by her arm. My muscles tensed. There were way too many innocents

121

here. If things got ugly I was going to have to find a way to get the big guy out of here fast.

Mystery Man shoved Keni into the nearest chair. "Stay," he barked around the cigar lodged in his teeth. She crossed her arms and rolled her eyes.

The bald, bespectacled hall manager scurried over, pushing his glasses up the bridge of his nose as he ran. "Excuse me, sir? I'm going to have to ask you to put that out. This is a no smoking facility."

The stranger said nothing … just stared.

The manager shifted his weight from one foot to the other. Visible sweat stains appeared under his arms. "You know what? We'll … we'll make an exception this one time."

Turning on his heel, the manager darted off for the safety of the kitchen. In his mad dash he bumped into Alaina, who glanced up and caught sight of our new arrival.

"Big Mike!" she squealed and sprinted over to him.

His stern expression broke into *almost* a hint of a half-grin as he scooped her up in a bear hug. "Little Lani, traded in the wings for a shiny rock? Never thought I'd see the day."

At the mention of wings, Gabe and I exchanged alarmed looks across the hall and rushed to intervene.

"It's been such a long time! I'm so happy to see you!" Alaina said in mid-gush when I walked up.

Gabe arrived at the same time I did and whispered in his bride-to-be's ear, "Maybe we take this greeting out into the hall?"

Alaina gave an enthusiastic nod and caught Big Mike's wrist. Before he budged an inch he clamped a mammoth hand around Keni's upper arm and yanked her along, too. "I wasn't sure you got my invitation, but I'm so happy you could come!"

"The Council wasn't going to release me until my presence here became a necessity." Slate grey eyes bore into Kendall, who squirmed under their weight.

"Became a necessity?" I asked as soon as we made it to the hallway. "Why, did the Council hear about the demonic stripper?"

"Demonic *what*?" Gabe's eyebrows nearly shot off his forehead.

Alaina cleared her throat and busied herself inspecting the crown moldings above the stairway. Gabe turned to me. His expectant stare demanded an answer.

"Want me to tell Alaina what the real draw of the owl themed restaurant is?"

"I heard nothing." Gabe relented and turned back to Big Mike.

"It seems," Big Mike's deep growl cut off any other further discussions, "little sister decided to give base jumping off a Nashville high-rise a try. Took a running leap off a twelve-story building without a parachute. Her little show would've had a nice sized audience, too, if I hadn't stepped in."

"They wouldn't have seen anything!" Kendall argued, her tone dripping with annoyance. "As soon as my wings were out I would've taken off and been nothing more than a blurred flash of white."

Alaina gasped and covered her mouth with her hand. "How did you stop her?"

The muscles of his shoulders rose and fell in a casual shrug. "Jumped out of a second story window and tackled her into an alley."

"Kendall, what were you thinking?" I threw my arms out to the sides, palms up.

The dramatic black and purple makeup caked on her eyes amplified her condescending look. "Unclench, Cee. It's seriously not a big deal."

"It seriously *is* a big deal," I hissed in an urgent whisper.

"This is the Conduit?" Big Mike jerked his head in my direction.

"Oh, yes! Sorry! Big Mike, this is Celeste and my fiancé, Gabe. Gang, this is Big Mike, my mentor."

Before I could open my mouth to utter a greeting he balled up his fist and punched me square in the face.

"*OW*! What the heck!"

"Huh. I expected the Conduit to have faster reflexes."

"I like him," Gabe declared through a Cheshire cat grin.

"I'm not a fan." I rubbed my nose and tried to blink back my tears.

Alaina ignored the socially inappropriate sucker punch and spun on Kendall. "Can you imagine if people would've seen your wings? Any attempts at normalcy would be gone! For *all* of you! Not to mention what you did was so risky that the *Council* felt the need to intervene. That should give you a clue that you aren't making the most sound of judgments."

Kendall's face formed a rebellious sneer I didn't know she was capable of. "I'm sorry, but did you get reinstated as our Guide? Because last time I checked you'd been long since fired from that job."

Alaina's lip trembled and tears instantly welled in her eyes. Anger flared Gabe's nostrils and puffed up his chest. "Kendall! I don't know what rebellious teenage crap you're going through but you need to *get over it*. Apologize to Alaina!"

Kendall gave a disinterested snort and started for the stairs.

"Hey! We're not done here! Where are you going?" he called after her.

"If I have to spend all day tomorrow with you losers I'm not wasting today here, too," she shouted, but didn't break stride. "Don't worry. I'm over jumping off of things. That was lame anyway."

This nasty attitude was so unlike her. What the heck was her deal? A sudden thought occurred to me that made my stomach twist in a painful knot. I had seen a transformation like this once before—*Alec*.

As the heels of her knee-high boots clicked down the ornate staircase I opened the channel to her emotions. Her warm glow still remained—which I took as a good sign—but some dark emotional drama she battled overshadowed it.

Gabe folded his arms over his chest and tucked a hand under each arm. His thumbs pressed against his giant man-boobs. "Think it's too late to talk Mom into only having two kids?"

"Maybe she's missing Keith more than she's been letting on?" I chewed on my lip and sincerely hoped that was *all* that was plaguing my sister.

"Don't mean to interrupt this touching family moment," Big Mike cut in, "but you know there's singing demons setting up in the hall, right? The lead singer looks like Eddie Munster."

"Of course there are," I muttered and rubbed my suddenly throbbing temples.

CHAPTER TWENTY

From the foot of the small, raised platform stage Gabe, Alaina, Big Mike and I gaped at … the Dark Army Glee Club. Grams and Mom led the rest of the onlookers in a round of applause when their rendition of *Girl From Ipanema* ended. The four of us by the stage didn't join in. Not that the geeky musicians weren't vocally talented. They absolutely were. However, knowing their dorky exteriors were disguises to hide the nasty demons underneath jaded us to the performance a tad.

"Eddie." I nodded to the Eddie Munster look-alike who served as the closest thing this band of misfits had to a leader.

"Celeste." He worked his eyebrows in an odd way that made me think he was either trying for an evil villain face, or he was gassy. I really couldn't tell which.

"Bold move coming here." I looped my fingers in the pockets of my shorts and straightened my spine.

"Straight into the lion's den." Gabe let his fangs slide out and curled his upper lip to show them off.

Red—a tall, lanky demon with shockingly red hair and the ability to actually *become* fire—gulped. "We're not scared of you."

Big Mike raised an eyebrow, the most emotion I'd seen him exhibit.

Red's hand shook as he pointed at our tatted up muscle man. "The new guy, on the other hand, is terrifying. Who's he?"

I gave a casual shrug. "We're going for a tougher image. Traded in the cute blonde for him." Big Mike pressed one palm over the opposite fist to crack his knuckles. "What do you think? Effective?"

Eddie's pasty skin blanched. "Very. Is it too late to get the blonde back? I liked her."

"Liked her so much that you tried to kill her?" I stared pointedly at the party responsible for that particular act—the demon in the back who fiddled with the microphone in attempt to make himself look busy. His blotchy, boil-covered skin hung off of him like it was a few sizes too big for his scrawny frame. When he attacked Kendall he grew into a globulous, mountain of a beast. Now he refused to look me in the eye. Go figure.

Hiding behind him were the twins. They were attached at the shoulder and completely identical. Matching bowl haircuts, small statures, and thick glasses held together by Scotch tape. Despite their weenie exteriors, they were a force to be reckoned with. They had the ability to transform into a giant, two-headed lizard with a wingspan like a B-52 bomber. Gabe still had a scar on his shoulder blade from a particularly nasty bite one of them landed during their brawl.

"She wasn't our target. Speaking of which, how is Caleb these days?" Eddie asked with his eyes widened in mock-innocence.

I lunged for him with every intention of delivering one well-placed punch that would rid him of his front teeth.

Gabe's arm shot out to block my path. "We have an audience."

The mic kicked on with a static buzz. Boil Face's surprisingly smooth baritone voice flooded the room. "How about this song during dinner to get people ready to dance?"

Together he and the twins launched into a full out chorus of *Build Me Up Buttercup*. It ended rather abruptly when Eddie unplugged their mic. "*You know that I have from the ...* HEY!"

"We're not *actually* singing at the wedding!" Eddie yelled as he shook the cord at them. "I just said that to get us in here."

"You really should have told us that before," one twin huffed and folded his arms.

"Like, maybe, *before* we worked up an entire song list," his brother declared and shook the paper in Eddie's general direction.

I utilized their distraction and opened my link to Rowan. A small taste of my emotions told him all he needed to know. He bowed his head, focused his gaze, and cleared the room. The entire crowd of innocent bystanders—Mom and Grams included—stopped their wedding tasks and filed out of the room like mindless drones.

Alaina gnawed on her lower lip as she watched them exit. "Uh ... Celeste? Quite a bit of the decorating is already done. And if you fight here ... "

"Oh, there won't be a fight," Eddie interrupted with a self-assured smirk. "We just came to deliver a message and have taken ... *measures* to ensure that we get out of here unscathed."

"Oxygen tanks have been hidden behind the speakers and amps. Two in the kitchen, one under the bridal table, one by the dance floor, and a few others scattered around the guest seating area," Red added and held up his index finger that glowed red hot. "One wrong move by any of you and I blow this place sky high."

"You're bluffing." I dipped my toe in to test the waters of that theory even though he looked serious.

"Try me." Red's thin lips pulled back in a grin that revealed small, widely spaced teeth.

"You're the Conduit. Why are you even talking to them?" Big Mike extinguished the stub of his cigar on the sole of his boot, and then flicked it aside. His hands curled into bowling ball sized fists. "Where I come from we don't negotiate with their kind ... "

"*Our* kind? What are you, a barbarian? We may be evil, but that's really no excuse for poor manners," Boil Face scoffed.

"How about if I apologize by ripping your head off your shoulders and grinding my boots in the sludge that's left behind," Big Mike snarled.

The entire Glee Club cringed and recoiled.

Eddie held up one hand and whispered behind it, "Where you find this guy? He's like a caricature of himself. Look into anger management for him. Seriously."

"Personally, I kinda like him," a familiar voice murmured behind me.

"Kat." This girl's habitual appearance at the worst possible moments annoyed me.

Gabe quickly pulled Alaina behind him.

"Another demon!" Beautiful bronze, tan, and white hawk wings slid out from slices cut in Big Mike's leather vest. His wingspan spread out twice the size of Keni's. He flapped his wings once and was on top of Kat with his face locked in a vengeful sneer.

I leapt into the air and spun into a sidekick that sent him flying back into the nearest chair. On impact the chair legs wobbled and threatened to spill him to the ground.

I answered his shocked expression with one raised finger. "I don't care what Council you work for. You're on my turf and you *will* simmer down. Call that payback for the sucker punch. How ya like my reflexes now?"

I expected a blow up of monumental proportions. Instead, a newfound appreciation calmed Big Mike's rage. He gave me a brief nod to proceed.

"Who's that?" The other Glee Clubbers moved in tight behind Eddie.

"Let me introduce myself." Kat adopted a sickeningly sweet schoolgirl grin that completely contradicted her black spandex bodysuit, and stepped into the middle of the crowd. Gabe rounded his back and growled, but she looked right through him—to the Glee Club. "You know the new force rising that your boss lady is just panting to know more about? I represent them."

Eddie's "geek" façade' fell away completely. Deadly steel replaced it. "She doesn't get out of this room alive."

Red's hands ignited into flame.

A raging inferno of barely contained violence brewed in Kat's eyes. Slow and easy her metal barb slid from her wrist. "And who exactly is going to keep me here?"

Gabe's features widened and stretched into an appearance more feline than human. A king of jungle rumble quaked from his twitching muzzle. He shoved Alaina toward me to keep her safe as he morphed. The twin's omitted high-pitched squawks of response. Their necks stretched and elongated as their own reptilian change began. Big Mike sprang from his chair fast enough to send it crashing to the ground and expanded his wings out wide. Everyone in the room struck a defensive posture of some sort—some significantly less menacing than others.

Alaina poked her head around from where she cowered behind me and grasped my Aerosmith tank top in both fists. "Celeste, think of the centerpieces! They can't do this here!"

I shook off her grip as Kat sauntered toward the stage. "Not really helping, Alaina!"

In a blur of speed, I intercepted Kat and grabbed her in a bear hug that pinned both her arm to her sides. "What are you doing?" I hissed in her ear. "Do you want to start a war? Because that's *exactly* what's going to happen."

"Get off me!" she spat and struggled against my hold. "I just came here to introduce myself. No harm in that!"

"And the flowers! They've already placed the flowers!"

"Everyone is going to get out of here in one piece!" I announced, still gripping a squirming Kat tight enough to leave marks.

Alaina whimpered.

In exasperation I tagged on, "Without harming any decorations or flowers!"

The resident Bridezilla heaved a sigh of relief.

"You've got something to say to me?" I glanced over my shoulder at Eddie. "Say it and leave."

He ground his teeth together and weighed his next move. The idea of taking Kat back to the Countess created an alluring prospect for him. The longing to achieve such a feat caused a sheen of sweat to dot his brow. Yet to accomplish that he had to go through me, which made that option considerably less appealing. I watched him mull the idea over for a moment before common sense prevailed and Eddie's tense posture relaxed slightly.

"The Countess wanted us to remind you of something. A little warning she'd given you about claiming your loved ones whenever the mood strikes her?" A wicked smile curled his lips and a victorious glint sparked in his eyes a second before they blinked to black. "Awful lot of family around for the wedding … Speaking of, no one close to you is acting *odd* at all, are they?"

His buddies tittered with laughter behind him.

Kendall. Ice ran through my veins. His threat and the possibility that it may have already come to pass sucked the air from the room. No one moved. No one spoke. The wall clock ticked off the seconds in time with the thud of my pulse in my ears.

Alaina broke the silence with a tone so dead of emotion it chilled me. She rose to her feet from her crouched and frightened position, her stare cold hard stone. "Celeste, let her go."

I didn't think, but simply acted. Kat charged the Glee Club with her barb poised for attack. Red and orange flames whizzed past my face close enough to singe a chunk of my hair.

The first explosion came from the kitchen.

CHAPTER TWENTY-ONE

Water streamed down the street and soaked my tennis shoe. Seated on the curb with my hands hanging limp between my knees I gaped at what was left of Gainesboro's beautiful library. Once a three-story masterpiece of sunshine yellow stucco, it was now nothing but scorched kindling and smoke from the second story up. The very structure had been weakened by the gigantic holes blasted in it. Not every tank had blown ... yet. The fire department worked tirelessly to douse the flames. As long as the heat was kept far enough away from the remaining tanks we would be spared another teeth-rattling, eardrum blasting explosion.

I'd never been inside an exploding building before. I wasn't a fan of the experience. After Red lit up two tanks everyone inside scrambled to vacate the premises. The Glee Club poofed off first—to the tune of Talking Heads *Burning Down the House*. Kat ran for the door with her arms shielding her head. In mid-stride she became one with the smoke and vanished as air. Big Mike grumbled and kicked out a window. He drew his wings in tight and stepped off the edge, plummeting straight down. I gave him the benefit of the doubt that he was going after Kat and not just abandoning ship with no forethought of those he was leaving behind.

A ceiling rafter splintered over our heads. Any second the roof *would* cave. "That's our cue," Gabe yelled and scooped up Alaina in his arms.

We sprinted for the exit and made it halfway down the stairs before the third tank exploded. The roof thundered down and sent a wall of flame surging after us. Tufts of tulle, flower petals and bits of decorations pelted down. I grabbed Gabe's arm and dragged him behind me as I slipped into super speed. I threw open the door at the bottom of the stairs and pulled us to safety. The three of us eagerly gulped fresh air into our smoke scorched lungs.

In exhaustion we'd collapsed on the curbside, where we watched through sore, bloodshot eyes as the fire department worked to save the treasured community landmark.

"The ceremony is still on track because that's at Grams' church." I winced at how raw and raspy my throat was. "We just need a new venue for the reception. Grams' backyard isn't huge, but maybe we could make it work?"

Gabe gently rubbed Alaina's back. "What do you think, Lani? We could get a hold of the caterer and just tell them the location changed. Wouldn't be too tough."

Alaina said, just nothing but kept her knees pulled in tight to her chest and her face tucked in the nest of her arms.

I wiped a layer of soot from my face then rinsed my fingertips in the small puddle by the curb. "It might even do Kendall some good to turn her loose on the decorating. She could have that place looking like a fairy land in no time and it might snap her out of her funk."

A muffled noise came from within Alaina's cocoon.

Gabe bent his head to her. "What, babe?"

"I said no!" Her head snapped up to reveal soft green eyes made more brilliant by the tears she silently shed as her dream went up in smoke.

"It's just a place, Alaina," I encouraged softly. "The wedding can still happen."

Her lower lip quivered and she shook her head. "It's not just the place. My dress and the bridesmaids' dresses were in there, too. I hung them in the ladies room while we decorated."

Gabe dropped to his knees in front of her and took both her hands in his. "I don't care what you wear. I just want us to start our life together."

"But what can that place possibly look like?" Tears streamed down her face, leaving zig zag tracks through the ash that covered her. "It won't be normal. Your calling won't allow for that." She jabbed her thumb in the direction of the charred skeletal remains of the building. "This is what happens when we try for normal."

Gabe brushed the hair from her face. Sorrow cut deep creases into his brow. "It may not be normal, but we'll be together."

"For how long, Gabe? How long will we be allowed to be together before some rogue demon lands a lucky shot that takes you away from me forever?" Her head fell. An auburn curtain of waves blocked her face from view. "It's just a matter of time. Love can't thrive in the midst of all this."

"That's not true." Even I heard the lack of conviction in my voice. But that couldn't be true ... because I didn't want it to be.

There was no malice in her voice, only pity when she murmured, "Oh yeah, Celeste? How's Caleb?"

Pain stabbed my heart and ground in so deep that it prevented any argument from forming on my lips.

"With an environment riddled with pain and violence love doesn't stand a chance." Alaina pushed herself off the curb and stared down at us. Rowan picked that moment to saunter up. He read the mood of the group well enough to keep his mouth shut.

"It's just a matter of time until that violence claims each of us in one way or another." Alaina looked first to Rowan, then to me, and finally let her gaze settle on Gabe. "Whether we submit to it, are pursued by it, or are overcome by it, one way or another none of us will get out of this alive."

Alaina slid her engagement ring off her finger. My mouth fell open and I felt my brother's pain as if it were my own.

Gabe's broad face crumbled in anguish. On his knees before, her he wrapped his arms around her waist and pleaded with her with every pore of his body. "Alaina, please don't do this."

Her shoulders shook from the impact of her sobs, but still she pushed him away and held out the ring. "I'm so sorry, Gabe. I love you so very much. But … "

He shook his head, denying both the words and the ring. "Don't. *Please.*"

"I can't marry you." She set the ring on the curb beside him and darted off, quickly getting lost in the sea of fire gawkers.

Gabe scooped the ring up and mashed it into my hand.

"Don't lose that," he growled. His features started to widen and take on a more feline likeness. His eyes glowed like polished topaz. Before the transition progressed further he leapt up and sprinted for the mountain range.

Rowan flopped down on the curb beside me and whistled through his teeth. "Tense."

I turned the ring over between my fingers, letting the light play across the princess cut solitaire. "If we can't have love or joy what can we have?"

I didn't even realize I'd spoken these words out loud until Rowan chimed in, "A pint?"

I snorted a dry laugh completely devoid of humor. "I just … I don't understand what we're supposed to be fighting for. I'm the Chosen One, by definition I'm destined for a world of crap. I get that and I accept it. But I never wanted that for them. I thought I could protect them from it. Take it on for them—somehow."

"Fate can only tear it away from them if they let it. Which—sadly—it seems they are." He held out his hand, offering me the relief I had come to depend on.

I stared at his offered hand and considered it. But in that moment I didn't need an emotional fix. What I needed was a friend. I felt him tense when I leaned my weary head on his shoulder, yet he didn't pull away. "No. For right now I want to feel it … and pray for a miracle."

CHAPTER TWENTY-TWO

"Think Gabe can get his deposit back on their apartment?" Mom asked while her finger trailed along the rim of her coffee cup. "It seems so sad for him to move into it alone."

At that moment we *should* all have been shimmying into uncomfortable formal wear and posing for umpteen-million pictures. However, no one had heard from the bride since the "incident" or the groom since he came home after midnight smelling of pine needles and wet cat hair and shut himself in his room. Wedding merriment looked extremely unlikely.

Grams pursed her red glossed lips. "I refuse to think about that. Those two love each other. This'll work out. I know it will. What do you think, Celeste?"

I drained the last of the sweet tea from my cup before answering. "I think the fact that her engagement ring is dangling off my Gryphon statuette upstairs is a bad sign."

Grams shook her head and brushed the crumbs from her bagel off the table and into her hand. "I didn't know she gave the ring back. Poor Gabe. I can't even imagine what he's feeling right now."

I opened my mouth to say, "I can," but quickly snapped it shut. That was a conversation I didn't want to start right then ... or in front of my mother. Instead we sat in silence and listened to the wall clock tick off seconds as we waited for—*something*.

ଓ ✳ ଞ

We tiptoed around the house and talked in hushed whispers most of the day. A chorus of honking horns interrupted our melancholy vigil around two o'clock. I pushed aside the curtain to see three deluxe travel buses parked in front of the house. The door to the lead bus slid open and out hopped Alaina and ... *Rowan?*

"Ah, crap. What did he do?" I grumbled under my breath and scurried to the door. Mom and Grams rushed out after me.

Alaina met us at the stairs. Her face gleamed like a freshly polished pearl. No traces of her sadness remained—which was suspicious considering her choice of company.

"Is Gabe here?" she bubbled. "I really need to talk to him."

Mom, Grams, and I all answered in unison:

"Is the wedding back on?"

"Are you getting back together?"

"If you hurt him again I'll break every one of your fingers and maybe a kneecap."

Alaina winced. Grams and Mom shot me surprisingly similar looks that seemed to question my mental stability.

"What? I'm just sayin'."

"I'd really like to talk to Gabe first, if that's okay?" Alaina's cheeks blossomed with the color of pink carnations.

"No problem!" The heels of Gram's wedges thumped against the wood porch as she darted back to the screen door and bellowed, *"Gabe Allen Garrett! Get your fanny down here!"*

Alaina's mouth fell open in shocked confusion. "I ... I was kind of hoping I could go talk to him *alone.*"

"Oh, of course!" Grams smacked herself in the forehead with the palm of her hand then opened the door and held it open. "Go on in, honey."

"Thank you, Grams." Alaina smiled meekly before she trotted inside.

Grams watched her disappear up the stairs before muttering out of the corner of her mouth, "Come on, Julia."

"Yeah, I suppose we could head into the kitchen and give those kids some privacy while they talk."

Grams crinkled her nose and gaped at my mom like she'd just declared animal print clothing should have an age limit. "Privacy nothin'. If we stand in the foyer we can hear every word they say."

"Even better," Mom giggled and the two disappeared inside. It occurred to me that Grams might be a bad influence on my mother—and the general population.

I turned my glare on Rowan and the entourage he brought to our doorstep. I narrowed my eyes and studied his face, wishing I were a mind reader instead of an empathe.

As I approached he shoved his hands into the pockets of his khaki pants and gave me his trademark smirk. "Something you need to say, *Mo Chroi*?"

I stepped in close and hissed through clenched teeth, "Please tell me you didn't brainwash the bride."

"I didn't brainwash the bride."

"Really?"

"No, not really." He laughed. "But you told me to tell you that."

"*Rowan!*"

"What?" Palms raised, he shrugged. Clearly he wasn't picking up on the line of questionable ethics that he crossed. "We both know she wants to marry the guy! I just gave her a ... nudge. A little boost back to the land of common sense."

My hands curled into claws and I fought the urge to throttle him. "You're messing with people's minds about life altering decisions. You understand that's wrong, *right*? I mean, I know you're thick headed and a borderline sociopath, but you at least *get that*, right?"

"We can stand here and debate the grey area of my ability all day, *or* we can focus instead on the fact that your little sis is currently shimmying her way out of your bedroom window. Your call."

I glanced over my shoulder. A lime green Chuck Taylor emerged from my window, followed by the other.

I groaned and rubbed a hand over my face. "Fine. But this isn't over. We're putting a pin in this conversation."

"Stupendous."

Rowan stayed put while I marched across the yard, then waited for her just below the window. Kendall shimmied out the frame on her belly and dropped gracefully to the ground below.

She turned with a victorious grin that quickly vanished when she saw me. "Ah, crap."

"Hey, Keni! Where ya goin'?" I chirped with mock exuberance. "And what the heck did you do to your hair?"

"Not that either of those things are any of your business—" she huffed with her newfound obstinate nastiness and folded her arms over her crystal studded skull t-shirt, "—but I'm going out and I dyed it black. Deal with it."

Her hair wasn't a pretty, glossy black, but the dull matte offered by cheap hair dye ... or *Crayola*. She may have been going for butt-kickin' goth chick but the combination of the hair color with her rosy cheeks, big blue eyes, and skin the color of fresh fallen snow resulted in her bearing a striking resemblance to a very specific *Disney* princess. If I didn't think it'd make her head spin around I would've pointed that out.

Before either of us could utter one more word that would've surely escalated things into a fight, Gabe and Alaina burst out the front door.

"The wedding's back on!" Gabe thundered and swept his bride-to-be off her feet to spin her in wide circles in the yard.

"What?" Grams feigned shock as she stepped back onto the porch. "Oh! It's back on! What a surprise!"

Mom followed her out, rolling her eyes at the awful performance.

In between giggles and squeals Alaina tagged on, "Oh, and you're all going to need to pack a bag! Rowan turned our wedding day into a whole weekend event!"

"You are such a sweet boy, Rowan. That is so considerate." My mom cocked her head to the side and graced him with a maternal smile. "Where are we off to?"

Rowan raked his fingers through his hair ... and blushed a little.

What the heck parallel universe had I stumbled into?

"It's a surprise. But a wonderful one, I assure you."

"As long as it's out of this Podunk town I'll be happy," Kendall muttered and stomped inside.

Grams put her hands onto her hips. The fabric of her coral muumuu drifted a little higher up her thighs. "I'm going to go pack and I'm throwing in a whole box of *Midol* for her. And what's with that hair? Looks like she should have seven little men scampering along behind her."

"I'm hoping it's a phase and we don't need an exorcist." Mom held the door open for Grams then followed her in. I took a moment to silently pray that the joke wasn't a reality.

More than a little uneasy, I veered around Alaina and Gabe's mushy-gushy love-fest of being lost in each other's eyes and stalked across the yard to Rowan. I needed answers and I needed them now.

"This is a pretty big thing you're doing." *Captain States-the-Obvious, that's me.*

He picked a fuzzy off his black t-shirt and rolled it between his fingers until it fluttered toward the ground. "Not really. I have resources and abilities. Might as well put them to good use on occasion."

"See, but that's the thing." I jabbed my finger at him. "*You* don't put them to good use. Ever. So what exactly is your motivation?"

He caught me completely off guard when he looked up at me with raw heat radiating from an intense stare. He moved in— body skimming close—and dipped his head down. Warm breath teased the delicate skin of my neck and earlobe. "Maybe I want you, Poppet. I'm hungry for a taste. And I knew that swooping in and being the knight in shining armor for your family was the only way to make you long for me as I do for you."

Blazing heat rose to my cheeks. I laid my hands against rock hard pecs (did he really have to be *that* buff?) and awkwardly pushed him away. "Look ... uh ... Rowan ... I ... "

He laughed as he played along with my shove and backed off about five paces. "Or, *Mo Chroi*, I knew the bird and kitty's break up made you sad, and the sooner I can get you back to being a blissfully happy Conduit the sooner I get to stop being your emotional *Band-aid*." He pulled a pair of sunglasses from his pocket and slid them on. "Now, I'm gonna go get a good seat on the lead bus and settle in for a nap. You may want to go splash a little water on your face before the trip. You look a bit— *bothered*."

I didn't know if it was possible to kick someone hard enough to knock the cocky out of 'em, but for Rowan I was willing to try.

CHAPTER TWENTY-THREE

Our chariots for the next twelve hours for all the wedding guests willing to make the impromptu trip consisted of luxury buses with leather reclining seats, individual televisions for each passenger, fully stocked snack and beverage bars, and on board restrooms. We drove through the night, lulled to sleep by the motion of the bus. The next morning the squeal of the bus's brakes and the hiss of the door as it opened woke me from a less than restful night's sleep. I craned my stiff neck to the side to stretch it after sleeping with my face mashed against a window for about six hours. After subtly wiping the drool from my chin, I stood and stretched then joined the crowd filing off the bus.

In no way was I prepared for the view that awaited me outside. The sun raised its head to the day in a celebratory explosion of perfect pinks, warm yellows, and streaks of brilliant orange as it burned away the light fog that settled over the sleeping earth. This provided a magical backdrop for the sprawling estate before us. I stared at the modern day castle with a soft grey stone façade, Colonial blue peaked and tiered roof, and acres of perfectly manicured lawn and flawless flowerbeds that surrounded it.

One of Alaina's hands fluttered to her mouth, the other clutched at Gabe's arm. "Oh! It's like the castles back home in Ireland! It's perfect!"

An elderly gentleman that resembled *Rich Uncle Pennybags* from the *Monopoly* game crossed the yard toward us with a warm smile fixed on his face.

"Welcome to the Biltmore Mansion. I hope your trip to our great state of North Carolina was a pleasant one." He bowed to Alaina and Gabe. "You must be the bride and groom. My name is Fredrick. I will be attending to all your needs while you're with us. If you would be so kind as to point your bags out to me I will deliver them straight to your suites."

Alaina raised her shoulders and beamed in glee. Gabe chuckled at his giddy bride then ushered Fredrick to the undercarriage of the bus that held their belongings.

Grams and Mom strolled by completely caught up in the history lesson Dr. Allyn, Gram's boyfriend, was providing about the mansion. Gabe's football players rough housed in the grass and playfully argued over who would have an NFL contract someday and own a house like this.

Kendall stepped off the bus behind me. She popped one earbud out of her ear, muttered, "It doesn't suck," then retreated back into her own little emo world.

Let them all marvel at it. I, however, felt the onset of a full force freak out. My gaze zeroed in on Rowan and I bee lined it straight to him. I interrupted his conversation with a bellboy by grabbing the sleeve of his shirt and yanking him around the side of the bus.

"Apologies, sir," Rowan nodded to the bellboy. "What she lacks in size and stature she makes up for with immeasurable rudeness and a complete lack of couth."

I ignored the jab and kept walking. As soon as we stepped out of view I spun on him. "This place is huge and has to be *unbelievably* expensive. You brainwashed them into renting it to you free of charge, didn't you?"

He interlocked his fingers behind his head and stretched up onto his toes. "Of course I didn't," he yawned.

"Good."

"I convinced them to sell it to me for a dollar." One side of his mouth pulled back in a lazy grin.

"*Rowan!*" I had never actually been stomping mad—until that very moment. "That is *not* okay! It's stealing and ... "

He dropped his arms and let his shoulders sag under the weight of my nagging. "Oh, please stop before you bore me to death with your incessant yammering. I'll give it back after the wedding. But in the meantime," he hooked his arm around my neck and steered me around the side of the bus, his spicy sweet scent enveloped me as he whispered in my ear, "look at them."

Gabe and Alaina attempted a waltz in the mansion's flower garden. Alaina tried to lead my rhythmically challenged brother through dance steps he clearly wasn't getting. He accidentally stomped on her foot causing them both to erupt in giggles.

"Do you really want to deny them this after everything they've been through? All of you fight, making sacrifices on a daily basis for the greater good." Desire darkened his turquoise eyes as he peered down at me. "But don't you deserve the taste of something ... sweet ... every now and then?"

My mouth suddenly felt dry and I licked my parched lips. Heat crept over my body like wandering fingers. I couldn't tell if Rowan was using his ability or if my hormones were betraying me. Either way, I suddenly felt a little *too* comfortable with our proximity. I ducked out from under his arm and put some distance between us.

"I don't need to taste anything," I mumbled, my cheeks burning bright. "What I need to do is to go get the super freaks off the last bus and help them get settled into their rooms. Oh, and FYI, if they weird out the common-folk be prepared to mind scrub the entire reception."

I scurried away without waiting for his answer. Lost in my own disturbing thoughts, and not watching where I was going, I slammed into Gabe halfway down the row of buses. "Whoa, sorry. Hey, where'd your lovely bride run off to?"

He fell in step beside me without even questioning our destination—a credit to his sentry calling I'm sure. "She was whisked off to an appointment with a dress designer. I was adamantly told I couldn't come. You, however, have to make an appearance at some point. Not to change the subject, but why are you all sweaty?"

"I'm not! Shut up!" I snapped then tried to reel in the crazy. "Just trying to make sure everything goes smoothly for your magical day. Did your friend Fredrick happen to mention where the guest rooms are? We need to get the guests lacking in mortality out of sight as quickly as possible. The less time they have to mingle, the better."

"Left wing, past the library and formal dining hall."

I paused, both eyebrows raised.

"I know, right? Keni isn't the only thing around here with wings."

We arrived at the third bus and I rapped my knuckles against the door. It hissed open and Sophia stepped out, followed by a tall, supple redhead I'd never seen before.

"Would you look at this!" Sophia gushed and flipped her hair to get it out from under the strap of her bag. "If I was ever to curse myself to a lifetime of endless monogamy I would want the party celebrating the end of my single life to take place somewhere like this."

"Uh … thanks?" Gabe responded and dug her other three bags out from under the bus.

"If you want to head to the left wing we'll be there shortly to help you find your rooms." I flicked my hand in the direction of the house, but was suddenly distracted by the death stare the redhead shot me.

"No worries." Sophia shrugged, seemingly oblivious to the unpleasantness of her travel companion. "We'll happily get lost exploring this place."

Sophia linked arms with the angry ginger and led her toward the estate. The girl kept her hateful gaze locked on me as

Sophia pulled her away. Out of spite, I refused to break the stare until she did. A split second before she finally looked away a reddish-orange light filled her eyes.

Before I could formulate any guesses on what kind of supernatural being the cranky redhead might be, the Grand Councilwoman descended the bus stairs. A magical illusion of some sort turned her normal feathered dress to polyester and gave her actual hair pulled back in a severe bun. I bit back a chuckle at the greenish hue that darkened her normally pale complexion.

She pointed at the driver in accusation. "That is a traumatizing form of travel! All those starts and stops! It's like daring your passengers not to become ill on the spot! I much prefer flying." Smoothing down the creases of her dress, she tried to regain a bit of her composure.

I gave her my best toothy grin. "So glad you could make it, Grand Councilwoman. The wedding just wouldn't have been the same without you."

"Well, obviously," she scoffed. Sarcasm zoomed right past her pinched face and over her head. She turned to Gabe with a bird-like twitch. "The Council is deeply sorry for the events that led to the relocation of your wedding. As our gift to you we will cloak the event and make it impossible for any demons to pass. We will make an exception for our host, Rowan, but are not pleased to do so. You are welcome."

Gabe held up his hands, palms out. "Whoa, whoa, whoa! First, you strip Alaina of her powers just for *being* with me, now you come here to make sure our wedding doesn't have demonic crashers?"

The Grand Councilwoman stifled a dry heave behind her fist and took a few deep breaths before she replied, "It seems certain members of the Council have deemed your impending nuptials as beneficial to our cause. As a traditionalist, I am not one of them."

"Sorry we didn't get your vote. I'm sure to lose sleep over that." Gabe's jaw tensed with aggravation. "So does this mean you're going to offer Alaina her job back?"

The Councilwoman straightened her spine to allow herself a better angle to peer down her nose at him. "She was sentenced to a punishment that is to be carried out in its entirety. Council rulings are only overturned under dire circumstances, which these are not. Plus, you have a superb guide in Bernard. Now, where is the bathroom? I need to vomit."

While Gabe muttered obscenities under his breath I took it upon myself to help her out to the best of my ability. I jabbed a thumb at the sprawling mansion. "It's somewhere in there. Good luck on your quest."

She pressed her lips together and strode in the direction of the entrance with determined strides. Figuring Gabe was sore after that little confrontation, I jerked my chin in his general direction. He gave a quick nod in response. In Gabe terms this was the equivalent of a heart-to-heart.

A cane thumped against the bus stairs behind me. I turned and offered my hand to the small, elderly man shuffling his way down the steep stairs.

"I don't need that, you nit!" He grumbled in a voice I knew all too well and swatted my hand away.

"*Bernard*?"

"Well, don't sound so surprised. I have magical powers, of course I could conjure myself up a more normal appearance." His hand dug into his pocket to scoop out some of his treasured berries and pop them in his mouth. I tried not to take it personally that he might have needed those just to talk to me.

Bernard's stature had grown to that of a typical little person. He wore a brown tweed suit instead of his usual bright garden gnome attire. His cane sunk in the lush grass, he followed it down and whistled through his teeth. "Would you look at this? Quite the elaborate place. Right considerate of Rowan, wasn't it?"

My internal monologue seeped out before I could stop it, "Sure, considerate. Unless there's something in it for him."

Two white eyebrows drew in and became one. "What would possibly be in it for him?"

"Come on, it's Rowan," I scoffed. "There's always an angle with him. Why is everyone so willing to overlook that and trust him all of a sudden?"

"It's not all of a sudden, Cee." Gabe stuffed his hands in the pockets of his khaki shorts and shrugged. "We learned to trust him—not *like* him, but trust him—because of how much time *you've* been spending with him. We just followed your lead on this one."

"I don't trust him! I was … " *Using him.* Guilt caught the words in my throat and made them burn like acidic bile. I was truly an awful person for how I'd been taking advantage of his gift.

"Whatever you feel about him, you've gotta admit this is a huge gesture." A look of resigned acceptance replaced Gabe's normal frown at the very mention of Rowan's name. "People don't do things like this for another person unless they really care about them. Plus, even if I think he's a tool, he made my girl all kinds of happy with this place. I guess that makes him kinda okay in my book."

Bernard folded his hands on top of his cane and leaned against it. "Maybe it's *you* that needs to be more open-minded about him, my dear."

I wanted to scowl and declare I had no intention of drinking the Rowan *Kool-aid* any time soon. But before the words found their way to my lips my gaze somehow found its way to the tall, tanned pirate who now stood by the entrance of the gorgeous Biltmore. He peered back with a stare so intense it made me wonder if he used his demonic hearing to eavesdrop on the entire conversation. Quickly, I averted my gaze.

I was thankful for the subject change Bernard provided when he drew the satchel that was flung over his shoulder forward and pulled a rectangular package out of it. "This is for you, Guardian. For the wedding."

Gabe accepted the gift and tore open its plain brown paper. Inside was a framed photo of our dad looking as handsome as ever in his EMT uniform. The warm and friendly nature of his smile made the gold flecks in his brown eyes sparkle. My brother just stared, and clutched the frame like a long lost treasure.

"I thought you could put it on the altar," Bernard kept his voice soft, a couple of octaves above a whisper. "So he can be here in some capacity."

My eyes misted over with tears as Gabe murmured a gruff, "Thank you."

Bernard nodded, clapped a hand on my brother's arm, and then hobbled off toward the front door.

"What do ya know," I mused. "Weddings soften even the most surly of gnomes."

"Even better than the berries." Gabe laughed, his gaze not budging from the picture.

The bus shifted as Big Mike maneuvered his enormous frame down the narrow stairs. He gave a cursory nod with his teeth locked around that ever-present cigar. If he was impressed, it didn't show. This dude was too cool to emote.

As he flung his tattered duffel bag over his shoulder he gave the framed picture a double take. "Huh. That must've been before he got his scar."

He strode across the yard with no further explanation.

"Wait … *what*?" Gabe and I both called after him.

CHAPTER TWENTY-FOUR

The tour of the Biltmore taught me two things. 1) Every room was more posh and extravagant than the last. 2) It would be very easy to get lost in this sprawling estate. Someone could venture off in search of a bathroom and never come back. The buddy system was going to have to be in full effect.

Frederick paused just long enough for me to admire the dining room with a sweeping glance. Wood beamed ceilings soared overhead. The hardwood floors were polished to a flawless gleam. A stone fireplace took up one entire wall with intricate pictures carved into its rock face. Two gigantic chandeliers hung over the beautifully ornate table that was large enough to seat two dozen people easily. Antique tapestries weaved in deep reds, golds, browns, and blues, hung from the walls to add warmth to the room.

From there we hustled through the library. Every wall—including those on the balcony—had built in bookshelves jam packed with various classics. The railings, crown molding, and fireplace mantel rose up to meet the ceiling with the most intricately carved woodwork I had ever seen. Plush ruby-colored chairs and couches were positioned around the room for guests' reading and relaxing comfort. Not that we took even a second to relax and enjoy it as Fredrick ushered me along at the speed of light.

My abbreviated tour ended abruptly when Frederick deposited me at the door of Alaina's bridal suite. To be perfectly honest, I'm not entirely sure what happened after that. The door flew open, someone muttered, "About darn time!" and yanked me into the room. Bony hands shoved me up onto a tiny footstool and I got barked at to stay. Mostly out of confusion, I complied.

The room looked like the residence of sunshine itself. Soft goldenrod paint coated the walls with accent trim in a brilliant white. The supple gold sating curtains and dust ruffle perfectly matched the paint. Two wing-backed chairs, the bedspread, and even the upholstered canopy over the bed were rich shades of brown with gold weaved through them. A table overflowing with goodies had been wheeled into the middle of the room. In the center rested a stunning arrangement of white roses and curly rods of willow. Around that sat every kind of cracker, cheese, or fruit a person could want and champagne flutes filled with sparkling lemonade. The decadence of it all made it look even more inviting. Temptation won out and I reached for a grape. A hand shot out of nowhere and slapped mine away.

"Don't move!" snapped a small, wrinkly old woman with an expression so sour the very idea of smiling would probably shatter her head. Thin, sandpaper skin made coarse from years of handling fabric clasped my forearms. "Stand straight!"

She snatched the tape measure draped around her neck and began measuring every inch of me. I sincerely hoped she was the person in charge of the dress fittings, or this was just awkward and inappropriate.

Alaina picked that moment to stride in from her private bathroom. "Celeste! There you are! I see you've met Helga."

"We've met," I squeaked as Helga goosed me with her tape measure.

The posh life suited our bride-to-be quite well. She plucked a champagne flute from the table and rolled the stem between her fingers before bringing it to her lips. An appreciative moan escaped her lips. "So, do I get to see the dresses I have to choose from or … "

"No!" The wrinkled old woman barked and hopped down from her footstool. She scribbled one last measurement on a yellow legal pad then stomped out of the room and slammed the door behind her.

A light blush warmed Alaina's cheeks. "I didn't mean to insult her."

"I think she works with fabric instead of people so no one catches on to the fact that she's the devil." Out of spite I plucked a handful of the formerly forbidden grapes and shoved them in my mouth.

When her moss green eyes widened to alarmed Os it occurred to me that jokes like that probably weren't well received by someone that grew up in the Spirit Plane.

"She's not a people person," I clarified as I chomped. "Not *actually* the devil."

Alaina breathed a silent *phew* and took another sip of her lemonade. Just as I picked up a glass of my own, a soft knock sounded on the heavy six-panel door and Mom poked her head in.

"Hello, Alaina." I knew that smile. That was the fake smile she wore in dire circumstances when she was about to snap. Nothing good ever followed that smile. "Your room is lovely, dear. Celeste, can I borrow you for a quick sec?"

"Sure." I set my glass back down and followed her out into the hall.

"You're talking through your teeth and that vein in your temple is throbbing," I pointed out as soon as the door clicked shut behind us. "I take that to mean the wedding fun train is rolling on."

Mom pressed her lips together and peered down the hall in one direction and then the other. Convinced it was all clear, she leaned in and hissed, "I don't know what religion Alaina's relatives are, but they're gathered in the Grand Foyer holding hands and chanting at the front door. It's not my place to question anyone's beliefs, but our guests are finding it a bit ... off putting ... to walk in and get chanted at." She gave my arm a quick squeeze. "Could you talk to them, sweetheart ... please? You know them better than I do."

So much for being stealthy with the supernatural stuff.

"Sure, Mom. I'll take care of it," I said with a tight smile and turned to stride off down the hallway.

"Other way, dear."

I spun around and marched in the opposite direction. "Stupid big house."

The low heels of the sensible, yet cute, shoes I'd been told to change into shortly after we arrived clicked over the polished wood floors and echoed through the cathedral of a hallway. It would've been nice if my black pencil skirt allowed me a longer stride, but apparently urgent matters were not factored in when this particular item of clothing was designed. After all the guests were settled, we were supposed to meet on the back lawn for the ceremony rehearsal immediately followed by a catered dinner in the ballroom. For the occasion I'd been forced into heels, a sleeveless white shift blouse that buttoned up the back, and the infuriating skirt that caused me to shuffle like a penguin.

Staff members buzzed here and there as they prepped for the wedding festivities. They strung rose and ivy garland down the hall, whisked candelabra centerpieces off to the ballroom, set up tables and chairs, and escorted guests to their rooms. I smoothed a renegade lock of hair that had fallen from the half-hearted twist and tried not to think about the knot of pain flaring in my chest. Surrounded by this spectacle celebrating the many facets of love I couldn't *not* think about Caleb. Pain sawed into my heart with a dull, jagged edge and caused my hands to tremble. It would be so easy to seek out the comfort Rowan offered, but that vice needed to stop. Now. Since admitting to myself that I really was using him it didn't feel right to allow it to continue. Six months too late I was finally going to deal with losing Caleb. I needed to meet the gut wrenching sorrow head on starting now. No more easy fixes.

Guests milled about in the massive foyer gaping at the splendor of the elaborate winding staircase where Grams stood center stage. "This staircase was considered for *Gone with the Wind* but we turned it down because we like to keep our anonymity. Which, of course, is why I never mentioned my connection to the Biltmore bloodline."

Despite my mood, I couldn't help but chuckle. I adored that crazy old broad. She had even changed into an outfit she deemed worthy of the Biltmore; a hat that looked like she'd plucked a parrot and hot glued its feathers to a beanie cap and a blue sequin dress straight out of the *Copa Cabana*. She shot me a wink through freshly applied fake eyelashes.

The reprieve she gifted me from my melancholy provided just the boost I needed. With a deep, cleansing breath I pushed my way through the crowd and even managed to mingle as I went.

"Aunt Mildred, it's so nice to see you! Cousin Connie! Have you lost weight? Uncle Lestor, you dropped your box of … toupees. Let me help you with that. Wow, that one's—festive. There you go. If you head over to that gentleman he'll show you to your rooms. His name is Fredrick."

Mid-way through the packed foyer the crowd parted. Some people tried to look anywhere except directly at the spectacle the Council members created. Others openly stared. The majority of guests scurried past as quickly as possible.

I ran a hand over my face and slowly shook my head. Bernard, Big Mike, the cranky redhead, the Grand Councilwoman, and Sophia stood shoulder to shoulder holding hands. Their gazes focused and intense … and seemingly directed at the front door. The rhythmic chorus of their chant echoed through the foyer and resonated down the halls.

"*Haud malum , haud everto , haud diabolus vadum penetro hic. Servo is terra. Servo is domus. Servo illa populus. Haud malum , haud everto , haud diabolus vadum penetro hic. Servo is terra. Servo is domus. Servo illa populus. Haud malum , haud everto , haud diabolus vadum penetro hic. Servo is terra. Servo is domus. Servo illa populus."*

The Capshaw's, our next door neighbors from back in Michigan, entered the house to that booming chant. The poor couple jumped and lost hold of their luggage. It popped open and littered the floor with their clothing and unmentionables. As they scampered to gather up their belongings I hooked my hand around Sophia's arm and yanked her around to face me.

"Oh hey, Celeste! Can you believe this place? This is like luxury redefined!" Her almond shaped eyes glittered with appreciation. She oozed femininity with dark hair piled on top of her head and a silky red dress that hugged her curves. I suddenly felt like a little kid playing dress up.

"Can the small talk. What's going on?"

Her eyes flicked to the Grand Councilwoman before she leaned in to whisper, "The Council needed the protection spell up STAT. For urgent situations like this it's always best to call in a muse. We're like magical amplifiers."

"Why is there urgency?" I asked through my teeth all the while keeping my fake smile in place for our guests.

"They didn't tell you? I ... uhhh ... " Her words trailed off and she gnawed on her lower lip.

After that she clammed right up, her leery gaze focused on her big boss. I took that as my cue to go straight to the root of the problem. I sidestepped around Sophia and used a little bit more Conduit strength than I needed to when I thumped the Grand Councilwoman's bony shoulder with the palm of my hand. She stumbled forward, her haughty glare at full wattage when she turned my way.

"I beg your pardon." Her words came out clipped with annoyance.

"What part of 'blending in' do you not get?" I pointedly glanced around the room then back to her with my eyebrows raised.

She pulled herself up ramrod straight and folded her hands. "I make no apologies for the discomfort of outsiders when I am acting in their stead to protect them."

"Protect them from what?" I hissed. "A fantastic time in a gorgeous mansion? 'Cause that's all I see you accomplishing here."

The Councilwoman peered down her nose at me. "Leave it to the Conduit of the Gryphon to speak about a situation she doesn't fully understand."

The redhead snorted a humorless laugh.

I crossed my arms over my chest and stared her down. "We haven't been formally introduced, you must be the Grand Councilwoman's lapdog."

The girl's nostrils flared. Her lips disappeared into a stern, white line.

"Terin," the Councilwoman spoke as if disciplining a naughty child, "do not let her goad you into reducing yourself to her adolescent, *human* level. We have a job to do. One she is currently hindering us from."

"Yes, Grand Councilwoman," she murmured in a husky voice. "My apologies."

They turned their backs to me and clasped hands once more.

My hand closed around the raven-woman's thin arm, no wider than my wrist, and spun her back around. "I'm afraid I'm going to need you to explain this job to me. Quickly. Before I revoke all your invitations and boot you out of here myself."

The redhead whipped around. Her pupils, irises, and whites of her eyes vanished, instantly replaced by red and orange flames that flared in her sockets. From behind me a few on-lookers gasped. It seemed Rowan would be serving a healthy dose of memory eraser as an appetizer for tonight's meal.

Terin's hands balled into fists. Her lean muscles were instantly taut and set on a hairpin trigger to erupt into violence.

I gave her a charming smile that dared her to make a move.

"We don't have time for this," the Councilwoman spat. She stepped closer to mutter for my ears only, "I gave you my assurance that this event would be free from demon attack. If you want us to uphold that promise it is crucial we invoke this spell immediately. Because, you see—you stubborn, obstinate girl— there are three demons on the perimeter of the property right … this … minute."

"Oh." My confrontational gusto sputtered and deflated. "Well, crap."

CHAPTER TWENTY-FIVE

"Wee-ooo, wee-ooo. Bum-bum-bummm."

Big Mike peered down at me with one eyebrow raised.

"Like in an old western movie? Good guys and bad guys squaring off?" His blank stare failed to register any comprehension at my clever reference. "High noon. Tumble weed blowing past. No? Nothin'?"

I missed Gabe and Keni; they might not laugh at all my dumb jokes, but they at least *got* them. However, my sword—Gabe—was currently being fitted for his tux and my shield—Keni—was busy trying to convince Alaina that black knee-high go-go boots would be appropriate under her bridesmaid's dress. Upon last check that discussion was not going well for little sis. That meant I had to settle for the next best options ...

Squish. "Tsk-uhhh!" Sophia lifted her foot and examined the grass and dirt caked on her sparkly red Mary Jane stiletto.

"Why am I here?" she huffed. "Muses don't fight! We inspire and right now I'm inspired to go back inside."

"Did you want to send me out here alone and unprotected? You remember that whole fate of the world thing, right?" I kept my gait steady and led the way across the perfectly manicured lawn toward the three silhouetted figures at the edge of the Biltmore property line. Truth be told, Sophia wasn't the only one wishing for alternative footwear. I missed my tennis shoes ... and the ability to walk without shuffling.

"Just seems I was the wrong choice. You were standing right next to the ... "

"Ah!" Big Mike grunted. He fixed his steely gaze on her, the veins in his thick neck protruded. "She wanted *you* to come, Sophia. No need to talk out of turn."

"Of course. Don't know what I was thinking," Sophia said with a tight smile, her lips pressed together so hard white lines formed around her mouth.

I couldn't have fought that eye roll if I tried. I was so over all this stupid, Council crap that they cooked up to validate their own self-worth. My only concern at the moment was stopping demons from ruining my brother's wedding. He and Alaina would get their happily ever after if I had to dismember a thousand demons to make that happen.

Huh, I wonder if I could find a wedding card with that *sentiment?*

I shielded my eyes from the sun and squinted into the distance. Light reflected off of a curtain of ink black hair on top of a lean form, next to that stood a dark, hulking physique. Kat and Trent. My pulse quickened. If the Council learned about Alec my chances of keeping him safe would become obsolete. They would order me to kill on sight. Sophia I could convince not to say anything, but odds of Big Mike keeping his mouth shut were slim to none. I slid my feet out of my heels and in a blur of speed—made insanely awkward thanks to my movement restricting skirt—I sprinted the remaining distance and left my cohorts in my wake.

Kat's readied barb welcomed me. Trent held up a hand to stop her advance. Beside them stood a ginger-haired boy of no more than sixteen. The freckles that decorated his nose and cheeks gave him the appearance of the boy next door—until he smiled and revealed a mouthful of razor sharp fangs. Once again Alec impressed and horrified me with his handiwork.

"Don't believe I saw your names on the guest list." I glanced over my shoulder. I still had a few moments until Big Mike and Sophia caught up.

"Guess our invite got lost in the mail," Kat snipped.

Trent raised both hands in a gesture of truce. "We're not here to start any trouble. Alec sent us to deliver a gift to the bride and groom. That's all."

My fingernails dug into my palms as I clenched my hands into fists. "On behalf of the bride and groom, we want *nothing* Alec has to offer. Now it's time for you to go."

Kat stabbed her barb deep into the ground and drew a line that cut through the grass and soil. "You think some stupid incantation can keep them all safe forever, Condu-slut?"

"Kat!" Trent barked, which garnered a twisted smile from the garish former beauty.

"Better hope none of your friends or family leave the grounds for anything." Her violet-lined eyes bore into me as she hissed, "All bets are off if they step foot over the line."

I held up one finger and smirked. "First of all, Condu-slut? Really? Have you seen you? Studded dog collars don't scream chaste virgin. Just sayin'. Second, I dare you to make a move on one of mine. I'll break that barb off and shove it up your ... "

"Celeste!" Big Mike jogged up, trailed by a panicked Sophia.

Gabe in mid-morph galloped up from behind them, tearing his shirt off as he ran, despite him still being on two legs fur covered every inch of his body. His mouth and nose widened and stretched to form a muzzle. Pointed ears elongated and emerged from within his thick copper mane.

"We can't find Kendall," he growled. His fierce topaz gaze shifted to Trent and his lip curled to exhibit enough fang to be an open threat. "Where's my sister?"

Dread caused my pulse to pound in my ears with a rhythmic thud.

Trent's chest puffed up as his spikes shot out. "I have no idea, *boy*. But you best step down."

Beside him Freckles gave his own winning smile.

"Little sister out here all alone?" Malicious intent oozed from Kat's smile. "Guess it's a race to see who can get to her first."

In three puffs of black smoke they disappeared ... and the race was on.

ෛ✳ෂ

I hammered my fist against the door without pause until Rowan flung open the door to his room. I'd seen the golden-haired pirate many times, many ways. But never clad *only* in a pair of black slacks that hung low on his hips with every inch of his toned and tan torso on display. Still wet from the shower, his hair clung to his forehead. I momentarily forgot why I was there and let my gaze sweep across the gorgeous tattoo that covered his shoulder and part of his chest. It was a pirate ship—of course—with shading and detail so realistic it appeared ready to sail right off his skin. I cocked my head and read the name, Marie Ann, etched into the side of the inked vessel.

"Can I help you with something, *Mo Chroi*? Or did you just come here to ogle me like your favorite dessert?" His moist and inviting lips pulled back in an easy grin, the desire that darkened his eyes couldn't be misconstrued.

My cheeks burned bright red and I purposely stared at the doorframe instead of the half-naked pirate. "There's no ogling," I scoffed. "I just hadn't seen your tattoo before. Not like I'd be looking for any other reason. Besides I only came here to ... uh ... "

Bad time to draw a blank. I knew it was important, too. *Crap.*

"Oh, for cryin' out loud." Sophia pushed herself off the hallway wall and swung around to stand beside me in the doorway. "We need his help to save your sister. Remember?"

My head snapped up with renewed purpose. "Yes! My sister! I lost my lion and I need a pirate!"

Rowan raised an eyebrow and raked a hand through his wet hair. Droplets of water fell from his hair and dotted his chest. Not that I was looking or anything. "Gonna need you t' take that a little slower and meat up the details a tad."

"Kendall took off and we need to find her *now-ish*. Before the band of demons currently hunting her beats us to the punch. Normally, I would take my lion for an outing like this, but since he's currently on his way to his rehearsal dinner—that all of us need to scurry back for—I was hoping to swap lion for demonic pirate. Will you help me?"

He gazed over his shoulder at his shirt draped over the back of a chair. "So, I wouldn't have to wear the monkey suit and there's the possibility of violence?"

"Absolutely. *You should put your shirt on!*" That came out more of a high-pitched desperate plea than intended.

"I wasn't aware you suffered from six-pack induced ADD," Sophia turned her head to whisper.

"Shut up."

She ignored me and addressed Rowan with a wide beaming grin meant to persuade. No one does persuasion like a muse. "We need you to do that nifty little demonic thing where you hone in on where the good guys are hanging out. Kendall needs to be found and brought back immediately. Big Mike and I will come along to help ensure her safe return." She wrapped her arm around me and gave my shoulders a squeeze. "And our lovely Celeste here would be ever so grateful for the help."

I gave her a sideways glance through narrowed eyes. "I thought muses didn't fight? Why are you going?"

"It's very important to me that the Council's orders are followed."

"Liar."

Sophia took advantage of the moment it took for Rowan to stride back into the room to retrieve his shirt and muttered out of the corner of her mouth, "Big Mike's hot, okay? Like insanely so. I'm just lookin' to spend a little time appreciating the view, that's all."

"Looks like Celeste isn't the only one with six-pack induced ADD, aye?" Rowan interjected with a smirk and shrugged his arms into his sleeves.

Embarrassment widened Sophia's eyes and turned her ears a fun shade of red.

"Demonic hearing, lass." He winked as he thumbed the buttons together. "I hear all." Shirt in place—*finally*—Rowan sauntered back over to the doorway. "And you, *Mo Chroi*, you think you can trust me enough to have me there?"

To an outsider it would've appeared a conversational veer, but I knew exactly what he was referring to. He had heard every word I said by the bus. I squared my shoulders and raised my chin. "I wouldn't have asked if I didn't believe I could trust you."

The corners of his turquoise eyes crinkled and that ever present smirk widened. "Well then, let's blow off the fancy-schmancy dinner and go save little sis."

CHAPTER TWENTY-SIX

The second I spotted my sister in the honky-tonk bar, my jaw swung open so fast it nearly unhinged and my eyes threatened to pop right out of their sockets.

Rowan's head tilted to the side. "How old is your sister again?"

I didn't bother to look his way, just stomped on his toe with the heel of my shoe. "She's sixteen, and you will be a pile of black ooze if you so much as look at her wrong."

"Ow!" He shifted his weight off the foot I crunched and scowled down at me. "While I normally wouldn't *dream* of eyein' the younger Garrett girl it's a bit hard to avoid, *Mo Chroi*. What with the sparkly blue brassiere she's sporting and her wings out for all to see."

"You can see that, too, huh?" I groaned. "I was kind of hoping that horrifying image was for my eyes only."

Rowan shook his head. "Nope, safe to say her audience can see and appreciate every second of her little show."

From her perch on top of the bar Kendall plucked the cowboy hat off a guy easily the same age as my mom, slid it on, and wiggled her hips in time to the Carrie Underwood song that blared through The Purple Cactus.

The crowd went wild hooting and hollering. With some fancy boot scooting Keni made her way down the polished wood bar. People moved their drinks to give her room—so noble and disturbing all at the same time. I watched Keni, my *baby* sister, merge a Victoria's Secret fashion show with *Coyote Ugly*. Keni shimmied down boob-to-eye level with a rather unsavory looking fellow that reached out to grab her.

Nope, not happenin,' Cowboy. I flew across the room, hooked Keni around the waist, and yanked her off the bar.

The surly crowd booed and hissed. Cranky Cowboy even hopped off his barstool like he wanted to start something.

"She's sixteen!" I snapped.

Eyes widened. Cranky Cowboy shifted uncomfortably, and suddenly he and the rest of her audience made a specific point of looking anywhere *but* at my half naked sister. *Good.*

"I'm fairly certain Mom and Dad didn't pay for years of dance classes for you to do *this!*" I jabbed my thumb in the direction of her stage.

A wry smile curled her blood red lips. "Unclench, Cee. I was just having a little fun. You should look into it." Her black shadowed eyes flicked from me to Rowan and back again. "You may find it ... *enlightening.*"

I bent down and scooped her black tank top off the ground and forcefully shoved it at her. "And part of this 'fun' I'm missing out on involves parading around with our abilities and attributes completely on display?"

Kendall gave me an "as-if" look and retracted her wings. "There. Happy now?"

"Yes." I balled my hands into white-knuckle fists to curb my impulse to throttle her. "I walked in on my little sister giving a peep show to a room full of people when we *should* both be at the rehearsal dinner. I'm friggin' ecstatic!"

At a maddeningly slow pace, that *had* to be deliberate, Keni pulled her shirt over her head. "The dinner sounded like a drag. Thought I'd check out the local haunts instead."

"Well your little field trip could've got you killed!"

Keni gave a disbelieving snort. "From these rednecks? Doubtful. We've fought, like, way worse."

Unable to hold back my rage, I grabbed her by the shoulders and dug my nails into her flesh. "Not from them!

There's a trio of demons in town that would like nothing more than to kill you because you have the unfortunate curse of being related to me! If we hadn't gotten here first they would've done just that. Big Mike and Sophia are outside right now making sure trouble doesn't follow us in here."

"They *were* outside," Kendall muttered and nodded over my shoulder.

By the entrance Sophia stood waving her arms over her head and gesturing emphatically for me to come outside.

"Ugh. What now?" I grumbled and spun on my heel to march for the door.

When Kendall didn't automatically fall in step behind me, Rowan seized her arm and dragged her along. "After we handle whatever *this* is I'll come back inside and give everyone here a good brain bleaching. Don't want rumors spreading about slutty angels."

"Hey!" Keni huffed.

"If the bedazzled brassiere fits, lass."

03 ✳ 80

From the other side of the glass door I saw a flurry of activity and quickened my pace. I hit the door at a jog and burst out into the muggy night.

Big Mike had Trent pinned to the ground with his arm at the ex-football player's throat. Trent's nostrils flared as he struggled to throw Big Mike off him. His spikes remained concealed, but Big Mike fought on borrowed time.

"Get off me!" Trent snarled through gritted teeth. "I don't want to hurt you dammit!"

Freckles pounced on Big Mike's work boot and gnawed on it like a dog with a raw hide. Not that Big Mike could feel it through the thick tread. Clearly Boy Genius was all teeth and no brain.

167

"Call him off, Conduit!" Kat's barb hissed free. "Or I'll give him a smile from ear to ear."

I let the strength flow through me—let it course and build. Then I gripped Big Mike's extended wings in both hands and yanked him back. As soon as he landed on his feet he kicked Freckles off him and lunged for Trent again.

In a blink I was in front of him. My hands slammed into his chest. "Stop! Geesh! Did they ever teach stealth on the Spirit Plane? There's a bar full of people behind you!"

Big Mike halted. His nostrils twitched and snorted much like the Bat-bull's had.

"Your receptionist has a serious attitude problem." Kat's black painted lips curled up in a venomous grin. "It was nice of you to deliver baby sister to us though. I'd hate for you to miss watching her die."

The tendons in my neck tensed to the point of pain. "You won't touch her. I promise you that."

She raised her barb and turned it side-to-side ever so slightly. Purple and green neon from the bar sign glistened off polished steel. "I'd love to see you try to stop me."

Big Mike and Rowan closed in tight beside me. Sophia grabbed Kendall by the shoulders and backed her away.

"Kat!" Trent thundered, his face set in a disapproving scowl. "This isn't why we're here!"

"Maybe it should be!" Hatred radiated from her glare. "I don't know why Alec wants to keep you alive, but I'd love nothing more than to gut you like a fish."

I stepped right up to her. Chest to chest. Close enough to smell the cloves on her breath and to get a glimpse of the gross mascara goop in the corner of her eyes. "See, that's the problem with being a minion; you always have to do what Big Daddy Alec tells you to do. He doesn't want me harmed. So, unless you want to be exiled by the only people—and I use that term loosely—who will accept you for the sadistic *freak* you've become, you have to toe the line and do what he says."

Her face turned red then purple. Rage twisted her tongue and made her incapable of giving a reply.

I gave her my best toothy grin and stepped back. "Now, you're gonna step aside so we can take my sister home. And none of you are going to make a wrong move in our direction, because if you do I'm sending you back to Alec in pieces."

Trent's broad forehead creased. He reached out in an almost pleading gesture. "Please, the girl needs us. Just give us … "

"She needs *nothing* from you." My tone left no room for argument.

He clamped his mouth shut and rubbed a hand over his baldhead in frustration.

I kept my gaze locked on Kat, who appeared to be grinding her teeth down to nubbins. "Soph, why don't you go ahead and lead Keni out of here? The rest of us will keep our friends company until you're out of sight."

Sophia pulled Keni tight to her then crept behind us and out toward the parking lot. She glanced back for a split second to give me a wink.

Out of the corner of my eye I watched Keni release her wings with a roll of her shoulders. Sophia turned and Keni hooked her under the arms for flight. Just then black smoke snaked past me. I whipped my head around to find its source. I didn't even have time to react. Kat solidified right in front of Sophia. Her barb ripped through Sophia's center with a sickening slurp. The blade jutted from Sophia's back. Blood dripped from the blade and decorated the pavement. Crimson bubbles choked up her throat and smattered her chin and lips. Kat retracted her barb and Sophia crumbled to the ground.

Lousy attitude or not, Keni knew what she had to do. She was already glowing with her healing warmth when she caught Sophia before her head smacked against the pavement. Big Mike expanded his hawk wings and met Trent and Freckles head on as our wall of interference. Rowan hooked his arm around my mid-section and whisked me to Kat in a cloud of smoke. He ducked out of the way just in time for me to swing my fist at her temple. It connected with a dull *thunk*. Before she recovered, I grabbed her wrist and shoved her down to the ground. Stitches popped along the seam of my skirt as I raised my knee to press down on her forearm. The barb was going to break. If her forearm snapped with it, so be it.

"You can't hurt me!" Kat snarled, despite her vulnerable position. "Alec won't allow it!"

"You're quite wrong there." The voice was so familiar it snapped me out of my red haze of rage. "Do it, Conduit. She acted against my wishes. This punishment is just."

Loose strands of hair lashed against my face as my head snapped up. "Alec."

I'd searched for him for so long, but now saw no traces of the man he'd been. Gone was the carefree cameraman with the long ponytail and laid back smile. A man with a sinister edge and a tailored suit that reeked of overspending stood in his place. His strawberry blond hair had been sheered short and slicked back. That, combined that with his pinstripe suit and he looked like a mobster from Hell.

Trent and Freckles immediately dropped down on one knee with their heads bowed. Alec didn't even glance their way. Instead he fixed his stern sapphire gaze on Kat. "You were ordered not to hurt any of them."

"Alec, I'm ... I'm sorry!" Her tough façade shattered and tears filled her eyes. "We don't need her, or any of them! Why can't you see that? You're more powerful than ... "

"Silence!" he barked.

Her trembling lips clamped shut. Tears and mascara streamed down her face.

Alec nodded my way. "Strike true, girl. And know that this soldier will not be armed again. Of that you have my word."

Something in the way he looked at me caused a memory to tease along the outskirts of my mind. A chill of unease shuddered through me. My mind screamed at me not to show the slightest sign of weakness. Not if any of us wanted to make it out of this alive.

With a bow of his head and wave of his arm, Alec granted me permission to do with Kat as I saw fit.

"No! You can't do this! I ... " Kat's plea transformed into an agonized scream when I brought my knee down sharp and fast. I both felt *and* heard the crunch of her bone snapping. The metal barb broke free from whatever connected it inside her arm and clanged to the ground. Her shattered limb hung limp at her side.

I scooped up the barb and hoisted her to her feet. The edge of the blade dug into her throat, but didn't break the skin ... yet. Even I didn't recognize the icy hiss of my own voice. "The only reason you're alive right now is because I know you're a victim in all of this. But if you *ever* lay a hand on me or mine again, I will *not* hesitate to kill you."

I shoved her at Alec who handed her off to Trent and Freckles.

"Get her out of here. Now."

The two wrapped their arms around their fallen comrade and vanished into the night.

"Impressive display, Conduit." Alec's gaze wandered over me. "I do hope the girl lives and it wasn't all for naught."

I risked a glance at Kendall and Sophia. A sheen of sweat covered my sister. Light radiated off of her, but blood continued to course from Sophia's wound. Big Mike crossed to them with determined strides. He squatted down beside Keni and added his own healing energy to the equation. I hoped it would be enough.

"We're drawing a crowd." Rowan jerked his chin at a few cowboys who stood near the bar's entrance and gaped at our bloody scene.

"Stop them before they call 9-1-1."

He focused his stare and the cowboys went slack. Like good little mindless zombies they turned and shuffled back inside.

Alec clucked his tongue against the roof of his mouth. "Such a busy girl. Saving the world really *is* a never ending battle, isn't it?"

A wave of déjà vu hit me so hard it made my stomach roll and my head spin. "If your kind would stop trying to destroy it maybe I could take up a hobby, like underwater basket weaving."

"My kind?" He cocked his head to the side and folded his hands in front of him. "Have you even figured out what—or who—I am?"

His arrogant demeanor was doing nothing to ease my nerves. I took a calming breath and tried to stifle my rising apprehension. "You're my friend, Alec. Or you were. And I *will* find a way to free you. That hasn't changed."

His head fell back as he erupted in a loud guffaw that echoed through the night. Rowan stepped closer to me. The tips of his fingers grazed my leg and a surge of confidence washed over me.

Abruptly, Alec's laughter stopped and he peered at me with deadly intensity. "Do you want to know the truth? To finally find the answer to this riddle that's been plaguing you?"

I squared my shoulders and met his gaze without wavering. "Tell me."

His eyes crinkled in the corners and a wicked grin spread across his face. "Oh no, girl. This I have to show you. If you want to learn what's become of your friend, close your eyes."

"Don't do it, Celeste." Rowan's chest puffed up in protective bravado. "I don't trust him."

Alec threw his hands in the air. His smile held firm. "What's to trust? The girl either does or doesn't want the answer. Keep in mind this is a one-time offer."

"I … I have to know," I whispered to Rowan.

He went rigid beside me, but objected no further. I dropped my hands to my sides and closed my eyes. Alec stepped forward and touched my forehead with one finger. The memories slammed into me like a monsoon of raging turmoil and emotion.

One blue eye. One black eye. The orchestra pit. A wall of scales rising higher and higher into the sky. Pooling blood. Bones cracking under a constricting grasp. Flames scorching skin. Lungs burning, aching for a breath.

I fell to my knees heaving and gasping for air. "*No.* It can't be true."

He gazed at me with a wry smile—and blinked. All the confirmation I needed appeared only for a split second … when his left eye turned black. "Our destinies are entwined, little girl. I'll be seeing you soon." With that, he vanished in an inky cloud of smoke.

"*Barnabus* … " I gasped and passed out.

CHAPTER TWENTY-SEVEN

"One, two, three, DRINK!" *Bam, bam, bam, bam!*

Glasses slammed down, rattling the table my head was resting on and waking me with a start. I wiped the drool from my cheek and tried to figure out where I was and what the heck happened. Judging by the bar full of rowdy, liquored up cowboys, I had somehow found my way back inside the Purple Cactus. My guess was that the flaxen-haired dude next to me doing shots with random strangers had everything to do with that.

"Aye! The lass has risen!" Rowan proclaimed a few octaves too loud. Clearly that wasn't the *first* drink he'd slammed. "Gentlemen, I bid you adieu as I tend to the lady."

The faces of the three rough and tumble cowboys went slack, drained of all emotion. Like puppets devoid of independent thought, they rose from the table, pivoted toward the bar, and marched away. Rowan even had the courtesy to plop them down on bar stools before he turned control of their minds back over to the rightful owners.

I said nothing, but shook my head at how he tiptoed around the moral grey areas of his power. "What happened?" I asked and ran my hands over my face to chase away the lingering grogginess.

"Well, it seems my ex-boss isn't as dead as we had hoped. You decided to handle this rather surprising turn of events by taking an impromptu siesta in the parking lot." Rowan's cavalier tone failed to hide the strain he felt. His eyes held the panic of a wild, caged animal and his incessant leg shaking caused the glasses on the table to shimmy.

Not that I could blame him. The news sank in my gut like a weighted anchor. I swiped a napkin off the table and rolled it in my fingers. "A nap seemed mandatory. I mean, it's not every day you find out that instead of just having *one* army of demons after you ... you now have *two*. All systems had to shut down and reboot to process that fun little bit of info."

Rowan raised his glass to his lips but paused before taking a drink. "Not sure Barnabus wants ya dead, *Mo Chroi*. Seems to me if he did, you would be. I think whatever he has in mind is much, *much* worse." He downed the remainder of his frothy beer.

"I should've stayed asleep," I grumbled and tossed the napkin aside. "Wait! Where's Sophia? Is she okay?"

Rowan wiped beer foam from his lips with the back of his hand. "Aye. They got her stabilized enough to take her back to the mansion. They were gonna recruit any feathered healers within a 1000 mile dimensional plane radius to come and amp up the wattage on her healing. I'm sure she'll be right as rain by morning. As for me, I have successfully erased any and all memories of stripping angels from every single person in this bar and we are free to head back whenever you're ready."

Back. I twirled the diamond and emerald ring on my finger and tossed that idea around. I needed to check on Sophia, but she was in more than capable hands—and back meant the return to flowers, dresses, and the big friggin' festival of love. On top of that I now had the fun task of delivering the terrifying news that Barnabus survived. Nope, not one part of that made me want to return any time soon ... if ever.

"Or we could *not*," I mumbled.

Rowan rested his elbows on the table, leaned in, and gave me a 'come hither' eyebrow wiggle. "What else did you have in mind?"

I rolled my eyes, but laughed. "Not that. Simmer down, sailor. I'm just ... not ready to go back to the real world yet."

He nudged my shoulder with his. "Fancy a dance?"

I turned to him with a mock look of shock and surprise. "Oddly enough mortify self in front of strangers was *not* on my to-do list today. So, I'll pass on the boot scootin', but thanks."

Rowan's warm breath tickled against my ear as he murmured, "You won't mortify yourself if you let me guide you. I promise."

He slowly grazed the back of his hand over my bare shoulder. I held back a gasp at the chill that started between my shoulder blades and shot straight up my spine. I was about to mentally flog myself for responding to him like that when I made the connection that his touch had prompted it. What a sneaky and unfair ability.

I scooted to the far edge of my chair. "No, thanks. I'm not really a fan of this song."

Rowan wet his lips and tried to suppress a grin. "Aye. It's dreadful. Let's see what we can do about that." He fixed his gaze across the room at the DJ. "How about if we dig into his secret stash of music?"

The record scratched. Country music stopped and inappropriate hip-hop pumped through the speakers. Bar patrons booed and pelted the DJ with peanut shells from the buckets on each table. The poor DJ ducked behind the table out of firing range, wearing a look that was a swirling mix of shock, fear, and absolute mortification.

I folded my arms across my chest and leaned back in my chair. "I have no idea what my 'azz' is, but I can guarantee I won't be 'backin' it up' any time soon."

Rowan threw his head back and laughed. "Ah, right. Fair enough. Let's try another." Again he tipped his head at the disc jockey. This time the hard-edged voice of Joan Jett filled the room. The cowboys approved enough to stop pelting him with snack foods. "What do you say? Care to admit you hate yourself for lovin' me?"

Despite my better judgment, I was actually enjoying myself. "Presumptuous and completely false. Try again."

Something flashed in his topaz eyes. Pain? Acceptance of the dare? Whatever it was vanished too quickly for me to know for sure. He peered around the room until his gaze settled on a woman and two gentlemen seated two tables away.

"There'll be no resisting this," Rowan said with a wink and fixed his stare on the trio.

They rose from their table and strode straight for the stage. The older man with the salt and pepper beard and slender build strapped on the guitar. His lanky friend with the handle bar mustache took a seat at the drums. The stage lights clicked on and the girl stepped up to the mic. Her white cowboy hat with its peacock feather band blocked her face from view as she adjusted the microphone stand. Then, mic in place, she tipped her head up. The light glistened off her cascading platinum locks like sunlight off of fresh fallen snow.

With a slow and steady rhythm the two men built a beat for her. The blonde's voice came out a low, throaty melody as she gave a country twang to Tracy Chapman's *Give Me One Reason*.

Rowan stood up and extended his hand. I peered at it as if it might bite. "I can't. Sophia was almost killed tonight. Not one, but *two* armies want me dead. Dancing is the absolute last thing I should be doing right now. Not to mention the whole sucking at it element."

He kept his hand raised. Its open invitation loomed between us. "Aye, and that is why you must. Once in a while you have to sacrifice what you *should* be doing for what you *want* to do."

"I *never* want to dance. That'd be like saying I woke up this morning with the burning desire to speak in public whilst naked. Not gonna happen." I laughed nervously and brushed my hair behind my ear. My hope was that my little joke would end the conversation all together. No such luck.

Rowan bent down beside me, his lips curled in a smug smile. "This is for your own good, remember that." He closed his hand around my wrist. His influence instantly removed any hesitation I felt. I argued no further and let him guide me from my chair.

On the small, scuffed up dance floor he turned and gently placed his hands on my waist. "Just trust me, *Mo Chroi,*" he murmured against my neck.

I somehow managed a forced nod.

To the beat of the soulful lyrics Rowan showed my body how to move. Slowly at first, my hips began to sway. The rhythm took hold and I churned in perfect time to it. Rowan moved with me, his body answering every question my own dared to ask. His hand wandered down and linked with mine. He drew me to him then twisted my arm behind my back and spun me out. With a little tug he brought me back. His arm swung over my head and caught me around the middle, holding my back tight against his muscular chest.

As the raspy-voiced blonde belted out a verse I rocked my hips side to side.

"Now you're gettin' the hang of it," Rowan muttered with a throaty growl.

I decided to give myself over to the first fun I'd enjoyed in a long time. I grasped Rowan's hand and spun away from him. When I glanced back, the desire that darkened his stare stunned me. It made what we were doing wrong—I had enough control over my own senses to know that. Yet there was a part of me that responded to him. For a moment I couldn't help but wonder what if ...

Rowan yanked me back with just the right amount of force. I slammed against his chest. His eyes were pools of intensity that I allowed myself to wade into. Nothing but a thin veil of energy separated our lips. With one hand he traced his fingers down my waist, over my hip, past my thigh and hooked under my knee. As the song wound to its close he brought my knee up and leaned me back in a deep dip.

Around us bar patrons clapped but it barely registered as background noise to me. A tumultuous inner battle of desire and guilt devoured me. Rowan and I stared at each other. We searched each other's faces, willing the other to make a move. Slowly, Rowan bowed his head to mine. I told myself to pull away but ... didn't. Instead I ran my hand around his neck and tangled my fingers in his hair to draw him closer. His breath warmed my face. Electricity sizzled between us, threatening to spark at our touch. Just as his lips brushed mine, I saw a bright red flash out of the corner of my closing eyes. I jerked my head toward it, and searched the crowd for the pale skin and crimson locks of the Countess. While she was nowhere to be seen, reality had just found a way to inject itself into my moment of insanity. The magnitude of what I had almost done slammed into me, the effects far trumping even the iciest of showers.

Forcefully I pushed Rowan away and sprinted out the door.

CHAPTER TWENTY-EIGHT

I don't know what I expected to find outside—maybe a talking unicorn that could fly in on a rainbow and answer all of life's questions for me—but what I found was sweltering night air so thick its oppressive moisture made me claustrophobic.

Rowan burst out the door behind me. "Celeste, wait!

I spun on him, fully intending to unleash an onslaught of ugliness even though I knew it would be directed more at me than him. Instead, I spoke the desperate words of my heart. "Take me to the water!"

He stopped abruptly a few feet away. His brows drew together in confusion. "What? What water?"

My hands trembled as I raked them through my hair. Caleb had never told me where our "special spot" was. But maybe the sea itself could make me feel close enough to him to still the hurricane of emotion raging inside me. "The ocean. Take me there, please?"

Rowan gave a resolute nod and closed the distance between us. His fingers laced with mine and my forehead fell against his broad chest. I squeezed my eyes at the disorienting rush that comes with transforming into a churning, rolling cloud of black smoke.

I didn't open them again until the heels of my shoes sank into the sand and salty sea air clung to my skin. I opened my eyes and gasped in crushing disappointment. Calming tranquility could not be found here. Not tonight. An angry wind slammed the waves against the rocky shoreline. From our vantage point on a dune ledge we overlooked the violent spectacle below. White water sprayed up with each assault. Birds seeking a safe place to roost for the night attempted flight, but found themselves at the mercy of the torrential winds. My hair lashed against my face hard enough to make my eyes tear. Somehow all of this seemed fitting. Caleb had been my peace and serenity. This tumultuous display represented my life without him. Violent chaos.

I glanced over my shoulder at Rowan. He stared at me expectantly with his hands buried in the pockets of his trousers.

"Why?" My voice came out a dry, croak that got lost in the roaring wind and waves. I swallowed hard and tried again. "Why did you do it?"

"Last time I checked, poppet, linking your hand around a fella's neck and pulling him to you isn't the sign for 'no thanks, not interested'."

I tried to wet my lips that had suddenly gone dry. "But ... *Caleb*."

"Caleb has been gone for *six sodden months*." His strong jaw tensed. His clipped words came through clenched teeth.

Tears of frustration threatened to spill. "I know that! But I can't even bring myself to take off his ring!" I held my hand up for him to see. In the cloud covered night the emeralds appeared a deep forest green, as if darkened by my almost betrayal. "Plus, you can barely stand me! Why would you try to kiss someone you don't even *like*?"

He cocked his head. Locks of wavy golden hair fell across his forehead. "Do you really believe that?"

"With the things you've said, the way you've behaved, and your history of selling me out to the enemy? I'm not the best at math, but I'm fairly certain that adds up to you not being my biggest fan."

He bridged the space between us in a blink. His warm breath tingled over my skin as he growled, "Then you truly are an infuriatingly *daft* girl."

"*Mo Chroi,*" I couldn't help the quake in my voice as I whispered, "I'm your burden to bear."

"Are you?" he scoffed with a dry laugh. "Caleb once told me you can read Gaelic, but can't speak it. That true?"

I nodded.

His gaze scoured the beach until he located a yardstick-sized piece of driftwood. He strode over and scooped it up. Stabbing it into the sand he drew the giant letters. Then, as his chest rose and fell with each ragged breath, he waved his hand inviting me to read it.

My mouth fell open. *All these months … All this time …* "Mo Chroi … *my heart.*"

His shoulders sagged and he tossed the stick aside. "Now you know."

I opened and closed my mouth, but the entire English language momentarily fell out of my head. Finally, I managed to stammer, "What … what am I supposed to say to that?"

A poof and he stood in front of me. He raised his hand rose to stroke my cheek, but he held back from actually making contact. "I want you to say that you aren't gonna tie yourself to Caleb's ghost forever. That someday—not today, but *someday*—there will be even the slightest chance that you'll open your eyes and see what's right in front of you."

"Caleb's not dead, he's … "

"He's gone, Celeste. Gone!" Anger darkened his eyes to a deep sapphire blue. His chest expanded with the deep breath he inhaled to calm himself. "For centuries now I've been driven by one thing, my need for vengeance … "

"Against who?"

"Tale for another day, lass." This time his smirk lacked any of its normal smugness. A hint of pain swirled in his eyes. "But even *that* vendetta I would give up to be with you."

If I were a computer I'd have that blue screen of death and a flashing Fatal Error message. "Rowan, my heart still belongs to Caleb. You have to know that."

His lips pressed together in a thin line. "Aye. I do. But I also know that there's something between us. Has been since the day that puff ball of a dog chased you into me arms. Can you at least admit *that*?"

The intensity of his gaze added pressure on an already stressful conversation. What I needed was time to think. Maybe a walk to clear my head, without him staring at me like he was trying to will the right words to leave my mouth. "This is all a lot to take in, could you give me a little time to digest it? Maybe think things over?"

"There's nothing to think about." He shrugged. "It's a simple yes or no. Is what I feel for you completely one-sided?"

I opened my mouth to say—something. No? Yes? I don't know? Stop pressuring me you maddeningly pushy pirate? But the words that found their way past my lips were, "I ... I don't think I can ever fully trust you."

He jerked as if I'd slapped him. Hurt and resentment fell on him like a cloak, sharpening the lines of his face and clouding his eyes. "I really wish you hadn't said that."

"I'm sorry. That didn't come out the way I meant and I definitely didn't mean it to hurt you." I reached out for him, but he backed away from my touch.

"You said *exactly* what you meant, poppet. So all this time all I was to you was an emotional release?" Even though I completely deserved the accusation in his tone, it still stung.

I wanted to retract my words. To reel them in and take away the hurt I caused him. But that particular skill I *didn't* have. "No! Well, yeah, maybe at first. But it became more after that. I don't know what exactly. But at the *very* least I consider you a friend."

He glanced at the words he wrote in the sand. The wind had blown the sand around enough that all that was left was a slight impression of what had been. "That's it then."

"That's what?" A terrible foreboding feeling hatched in my belly. Rowan's posture suddenly went *too* rigid. The muscles in his arms and neck became *too* taut. "You put me on the spot. I'm sorry if I said something wrong. I truly didn't mean to hurt you."

"I didn't want it to be like this." Slowly and deliberately—like a predatory cat—he slunk toward me. The dark intensity of his gaze made the hair on the back of my neck stand on end. "I was never going to follow through. I thought when the time came I would be able to sway you. But you just can't see past that sodding Irishman."

Instinctively my hands balled into fists. "Rowan, whatever you're thinking of doing right now—*don't*."

"All you had to do was give me *one* reason not to go through with it. But now it's too late."

His behavior was so erratic I didn't know what to expect. I absolutely was *not* prepared for him to weave his fingers into my hair and kiss me with a fierce intensity that took my breath away. An intoxicating rush of lust-filled heat raged into me the second his lips touched mine. Completely at the mercy of this invading emotion I wrapped my arms around his neck and molded my body to him. I was so caught up in his tongue teasing mine that I didn't even notice when our corporeal forms turned into black smoke ...

CHAPTER TWENTY-NINE

I didn't know where he transported, and honestly I was too distracted to care. My hands wandered up Rowan's back, enjoying the feel of him. With one arm around my waist he roughly pulled me to him. A throaty groan I didn't know I was capable of escaped through my parted lips. His mouth never left mine as he guided me across the room until my back smacked into what I assumed to be a wall. Not that I cared, I was in the middle of loosening the buttons of his shirt. Rowan caught one of my hands and in a swift, sudden motion brought it down and clamped a metal cuff around my wrist.

Nothing snaps a girl out of a manufactured lusty vibe faster than finding herself involuntarily bolted to a heavy wood slab.

"What are you doing?" I growled and yanked against the cuff. Whatever this thing was made of it didn't even budge at my attempt.

Rowan's hand rose to stroke my cheek. I flinched away from him. My breath came fast and ragged in my sudden blinding fury. Sadness flared in his eyes that he quickly blinked away. Stone cold resolve replaced it and he clapped his hand down on my arm. He compelled my other arm down with his touch and clicked the second cuff in place.

"I never wanted this, Celeste." He *tsk*ed and shook his head. "I thought once Caleb was gone, things would be different."

I lunged at him. Unfortunately, he stepped out of head-butting range. "Tell me you didn't have anything to do with me having to send Caleb away."

He turned on his heel and strode across the room muttering under his breath, "Bolted to a sodding table and still she thinks of him first."

"Answer my question," I snarled and scanned my surroundings for a weak spot to bolt through. Even if I found a door with a well-lit EXIT sign I wasn't going anywhere thanks to these cuffs made of some sort of Conduit-proof kryptonite. I had to be somewhere inside the mansion. The room had the same high ceilings and beautiful cherry-stained, wood-paneled walls. Antique candelabras lit the space with their warm candlelit glow. Positioned in the middle of the room was an ornate antique table with three knives on it. One with a mother of pearl hilt, one with black onyx, and the last polished brass. Next to them sat a copper bowl and a red candle. When the only two pieces of furniture in a room are a table full of knives and a table with handcuffs it's safe to assume a spa treatment isn't on the docket.

The soft light of the candles provided no match for the inferno that burned in Rowan's gaze when he spun on me. "Did I have something to do with it? You're damned right I did. I was protecting him from *you*. If he had stayed here sooner or later the Countess would've gotten her payback and had him killed. He's the only family I've ever had. To keep him safe I had to get him far away from *you*."

Metal gleamed as Rowan picked up the black onyx knife and turned it over in his hands. Studying it. Weighing it. Slowly he drew the edge of the blade down his palm. A crimson line split his hand. Over the bowl he made a fist and let the blood stream down.

"That's why you were on the island." A fresh round of boiling rage prompted me to jerk against my chains with the same end result. "You led the Titan right to us."

He peered up at me. A lock of golden hair fell into his eye. He flicked his head to adjust it. "I did. But I never meant for anyone to get hurt—the exact opposite in fact. I care for you and Cal both dearly and I hoped it wouldn't come to this. If you gave me one hint—one inkling—that you cared for me I would've kept you safe. "

"Safe from *what*? What could possibly be worse than *you*? You lying, scheming, villainous, untrustworthy *pirate!*" I spat. Thanks to him that was now the worst possible word in my vocabulary.

The hangdog expression he wore while he wrapped a handkerchief around his still bleeding hand kinda made me wanna jab my thumbs in his eyes. "If you live through this I do hope you'll forgive me someday."

"Don't count on it," I hissed.

Rowan gave an almost sympathetic nod, but said nothing. Instead he scooped up the red candle and lit it off the nearest candelabra. Holding it over the bowl, he let the melted wax run down the length of the pillar and drip into the bowl. "*Sanus exsisto clausus , ianua exsisto sterilis , servo is tractus.*"

I had a feeling this particular chant wasn't going to end with unicorns and cotton candy. My muscles tensed, ready for anything but able to do shockingly little at the moment. "Whatever you're doing, Rowan, you don't have to. If you meant any of those things you said about how you feel about me, don't do this."

The smoke from the candle grew thick and heavy. Grey smog filled the room and burned my lungs with its spicy sweetness. Rowan kept his head down, and watched the wax drip and splatter in the copper bowl. "For centuries the only thing driving me to stay alive was a vendetta I've harbored for way longer than a sane man should. But meeting you and watching what you've endured made it seem—pointless. My own pains from the past paled in comparison to what you endure daily. The strength you possess, the compassion that defines you—it's what made me long to be near you." I saw no accusation in his eyes, only truth, when he peered up at me from under his lashes. "But it isn't me you want, it never has been. So if my past goal is all I have left, I have no choice but to pursue it."

Out of options, I opened the channel between us. I felt his swirling vortex of empty pain and anguish. Hopeless rejection courtesy of me. Quickly, I broke the link. Rowan was doing this because he felt he had nothing left. As red-rage, teeth gnashing ticked as I was, I didn't want this for him. We had been friends—kind of—and he was about to destroy that. However, I had the advantage of *knowing* he still cared for me and that gave me something to build on.

"Rowan," I concentrated on keeping my tone soft, calm, and controlled. "It's not too late. Please, let me go. Undo whatever this is."

Behind me wood *swooshed* over wood, like a pocket door slid open. I turned my head as far as possible, but the table blocked my view.

"Oh, I'm afraid we're way past that point, my dear."

Recognition of that voice caused icy terror to seep through my veins. "*Bernard.*"

CHAPTER THIRTY

Relying heavily on his cane Bernard *shuffled-thumped* into my line of sight. Yet the sound didn't stop when he halted in front of me. Instead it intensified, growing to a loud drumming chorus that filled the room. *Shuffle-thump, shuffle-thump, shuffle-thump, shuffle-thump, shuffle-thump, shuffle-thump, shuffle-thump, shuffle-thump, shuffle-thump, shuffle-thump.*

I choked on my scream. If someone ripped my worst nightmare directly from my head and showed it to me, this would be it. Before me stood a gaggle of roughly a hundred gnomes.

"Rowan," I gasped in a high-pitched 'I'm-about-to-have-the-mother-of-all-freak-outs' wheeze. "Here's a little known fact about me. This ... " chains rattled as I waved a shackled hand at the gnomes, " ... is quite literally one of my biggest phobias come to life."

Some gnomes exchanged confused looks, others puffed up their wee little chests in acts of cocky bravado. Rowan gave a slightly bewildered snort of amusement.

My eyebrows nearly rocketed off my face. "Oh, I'm not kidding. I'm seconds away from a freak out that will forever change the way you look at me. *Seriously*. I am begging you—flat out *begging* you. Get me out of here. *Please*."

Flaxen brows drew together as the intensity of my plea registered with the pirate. He glanced around at the plethora of tiny folk that should've been guarding flowerbeds across the lands instead of whatever bout of nastiness they intended to inflict. Yet before he could lift one finger to help, Bernard took preventative measures to stop just that.

"Rowan will do no such thing. We had a deal, sir." Bernard hobbled over to him, dug into the satchel thrown across his chest, and pulled out a rolled scroll with wooden handles at each end. He unrolled it with great flourish to reveal a detailed map. Rowan sucked in air through pursed lips. With a smug nod Bernard handed it over. "As you can see this is your payment in full."

I yanked against my chains as hard as my super strength would allow. "A map? You sold me out for a map? Is it directions on how to crawl up your own butt and die? Because it *really* should be."

Deep yearning darkened Rowan's topaz eyes as he gazed at the worn parchment. Earlier tonight he'd looked at me that same way. Now I was strapped to a table. I couldn't help but wonder if the map would fare better. "This will help me find my dear Marie Ann. The one girl that never let me down but was viciously stolen from me."

Marie Ann? Why did that sound familiar? Then it hit me. My eyes narrowed with contempt and outrage. "Your tattoo. Marie Ann is a friggin' *boat*!"

Rowan rolled the map up tight. A smug smile spread across his annoyingly handsome face. "A ship, dearie. I told ya I'd get back to the sea someday."

"Stop talking," I huffed. "Every word you utter is making me hate you more."

He gave a suit-yourself shrug he shifted his gaze to Bernard. "Promise me she won't be hurt."

"Oh, *now* you care about my well-being?" I scoffed and shook my head. "We need to look into getting you a cute little cartoon cricket for a conscience, because I think what you have now is a decomposing parrot."

"We plan to suck the power from her, boy." Bernard ignored me and raised his berry-stained hand in the air palm up. "There's a high likelihood that'll smart."

"Aye. Right and fair, but you won't be killin' her?"

Bernard's peach-sized head turned my way. "As long as she doesn't do anything stupid we won't hurt her. But, let's be honest, it's Celeste. She's bound to do something stupid."

"I get my hands on your cane and I'll show you stupid, you little beady-eyed twerp!" I lunged for him, but stopped when the chains nearly dislocated my shoulders.

Four gnomes flanked me, two on each side. They folded their arms over their chests and peered up at me from under furrowed white-caterpillar eyebrows. I couldn't have stifled that cringe or prevented my impromptu whimper if I wanted to. This was too much creepy at way too intimate a proximity.

"I want your word you won't kill her," Rowan demanded.

"And I'll give ya no such thing!" Bernard slammed his cane against the floor to punctuate his declaration. "You named your price, and it's been met. If the girl's safety was an issue it should've been established when we discussed your payment."

Rowan rocked back on his heels and rolled the map between his hands. "You're absolutely right, mate. A deal's a deal. I handed her over and you kept up your end of the deal. Our business here is through, wouldn't you say?"

Bernard waved his hand as if to swat the words away. "Yes, yes, pirate guidelines and all that. Our deal is complete and you're free to go."

"Then go I shall." Rowan tucked the map into the back waistband of his pants and shot me a wink. "Best of luck, poppet."

"*Don't you dare leave me here!* Help *me!*" I hollered loud enough to strain my vocal cords. But my shout only reached a black cloud of smoke.

"I should probably tell you this now, Celeste." Bernard's voice dripped with condescension. "You can scream all you want, no one outside of these walls will hear you. And even if they did, none can enter. The spell I had Rowan cast ensured that."

Rowan's lingering black cloud distracted me from Bernard's pompous gnome drivel. It swirled around the room in a

191

mini-cyclone. Some gnomes held on to their hats. Other's scurried after theirs when they went airborne. White, bushy beards blew into gnome faces and left them sputtering to breathe through their own hair. I turned my face away from the powerful gusts as the cloud blew my way. The winds caused my skirt to creep up my thighs and twisted my hair into unruly knots.

In the midst of it a ghost-hand brushed my cheek and a disembodied voice murmured in my ear, "Break the bowl, *Mo Chroí*. The room will no longer be bound."

The wind abruptly stopped and he disappeared.

My gaze locked on the bowl. One telekinetic shove should do the trick. But then what? I'd still be shackled to a table surrounded by a herd of seriously peeved gnomes. That horrifying image made me pause and hope that a better opportunity would present itself—*quickly*.

Bernard shoved a handful of berries in his mouth, clapped his hands together, and peered at me with glee. Deep wine-colored juice dribbled from his lips and stained his white beard pink. "Let's get to work, fellas!"

All around me tiny men sprang into action. Metal screeched as the table I was on lowered back. Gnomes busily buzzed around. What they were doing I could only imagine. My view was restricted to the occasional glimpse of pointy red, blue, and yellow hats that bobbed past the table.

"So what's the plan here, Bernie?" My voice cracked with fear and I struggled to steady it. "Wanna drain my powers and take my place as the Conduit, do ya? Seems there would be an easier way to get a promotion like that."

"You think I have the desire to be nothing more than a receptacle to borrowed powers?" Bernard's voice seemed more sinister as nothing more than a faceless echo. "Hardly. I will harness your power and then hand it over to my true Master. Then she will finally be able to seek the vengeance she longs for against the Gryphon."

"The Countess," I muttered to the ceiling.

Around me all motion halted. Fifty voices dreamily crooned, "The Countess."

"Figures," I grumbled in disgust.

If Rowan knew about Bernard's connection to the Countess I would take great joy in killing him—if I ever got out of this room. But honestly, I should've known. The second she gave me a "tip" about Caleb and the Titans I should've guessed it all tied together in a way that served *her* greater good. She needed Caleb out of the way so her boy Bernard could encourage Rowan to move in. That was one chick that was begging to get her teeth kicked in.

"Any chance her royal sluttiness is going to be making a personal appearance tonight?"

A collective hiss filled the room from shocked and appalled gnomes.

"You are not worthy to lay eyes on her!" Bernard boomed.

I snorted a humorless laugh and let my head fall against the table. "Aaannnd she can't step foot on the property because of the spell the Council cast. For a diabolical villain your boss is kind of an asshat."

"Do not speak ill of her magnificence!" Bernard pointed his cane and electricity rocketed through my body.

My head rose up as the electricity tensed my neck muscles. When the current stopped my noggin smacked against the table hard enough to bounce. I thrashed with enough force to draw blood against the metal cuffs. The small wounds should've healed instantly, but whatever the cuffs were made of hindered that as well.

"The blood! We must catch the blood!" a soft, squeaky voice declared. Feet scurried across the floor. A moment later the bronze bowl appeared at the edge of the table to catch the small stream of blood that trickled from my wrist.

Bernard's voice bubbled with jubilance. "It has begun! Nicholi, Astor, retrieve the pearl handled knife. A shallow cut to each of her arms and legs. Catch every drop of blood that falls.

Bring me the bronze knife so I may add my own blood to the mix. Hurry now!"

Foggy headed from the jolt I stared up at the crystal chandelier and tried to regain focus. The teardrop shaped crystals seemed oddly appropriate for the circumstances.

"So she gets all this power and revenge. Where does that leave you, Bernard?" I croaked, my throat painfully dry and parched. "An outcast to the Council you swore to serve and protect?"

A silver blade poked up over the edge of the table. It appeared to float thanks to the limited reach of the tiny hand that wielded it. It came down in a smooth, quick motion that sliced into my left leg just above my ankle. I gritted my teeth through the pain. These little jerks wouldn't get the satisfaction of hearing me scream.

"With the Gryphon defeated the Council will soon follow." Bernard's voice was tight with pain. He must've started his portion of the blood ritual. "They will pledge their allegiance to her Most Radiance or they will die horribly. We will be by her side until the very end, to see her claim her victory and begin her reign."

A second slash sliced my opposite ankle, then a third to my wrist. I grimaced and fought for freedom against my restraints. "Minions for all eternity? Way to shoot for the bottom of the food chain."

"Say what you will, girl," Bernard chuckled, "soon you will be nothing more than a useless mortal. If our Royal Beauty feels generous when her reign begins she may have you enslaved for the remainder of your days. If not, you'll be killed. Being a minion doesn't sound so bad compared to that, now does it?"

The knife sliced through my flesh for a fourth time. Any witty comments I had were squelched by my need to stifle an involuntary yelp that threatened to escape.

Bernard snapped his fingers. "The scepter. Now."

An opalescent blue globe mounted to a decorative golden rod bobbed by the table. The marionette show of odd floating items may've been downright comical if the circumstances weren't so bleak and dire.

A plan would be nice, but I had nothin'. Scream? Send out an urgent empathic SOS? Both options were useless since no one could get in—or even hear me. I could break the bowl to allow my crew access, but that would start a gnome tizzy. If back up didn't burst in immediately the pint-sized army would slaughter me. Not the most heroic way for the Chosen One to go out—yet definitely the most terrifying. Checking one and then the other, I pulled my hands off the table and inspected the shackles for a loose screw or rusty bolt I could telekinetically remove. They were solid with all shiny new hardware. Probably reinforced just for me. How thoughtful.

The scepter popped up by my feet, brandished high by a berry-stained hand. "Silence! It's time!"

When all else fails, stall for time. "This is gonna end badly for you, Bernie. The Council will have your head. Offering up the Chosen One as a sacrifice? That ranks high on their list of big time no-no's."

Bernard ignored me and raised the scepter high. "*Contraho. Illustro. Recolligo. Aufero.* Gather here! Join me, brothers!"

Their voices raised in a child-like chorus, "*Contraho. Illustro. Recolligo. Aufero. Contraho. Illustro. Recolligo. Aufero. Contraho. Illustro. Recolligo. Aufero. Contraho. Illustro. Recolligo. Aufero.*"

A soft glow began in my chest that quickly grew and spread over my entire body. With it came the most excruciating pain I'd ever experienced. My back arched off the table and a gut-wrenching wail tore from my throat. The intense pressure made me feel my insides tried to burst through my skin. If this was my powers being forcibly ripped out of me then it seemed the very fibers of my being weren't letting go without a fight. I felt the strength leaving my body, being sucked out of me like dust up a vacuum. Life itself slipped from my grasp, along with my powers. At this rate the gnomes would snuff me out like a candle that once burned bright in a matter of seconds. The fight left my body and I slammed down on the table reduced to nothing but dead weight. My vision swam out of focus. The room spun and churned in a fun house effect. I tried to extend my fingers but couldn't budge them from their claw-like position.

"*Contraho. Illustro. Recolligo. Aufero. Contraho. Illustro. Recolligo. Aufero. Contraho. Illustro. Recolligo. Aufero. Contraho. Illustro. Recolligo. Aufero.*"

The pain that I thought couldn't get any worse amplified to a whole new level. I gaped down sure a dagger had plunged into my rib cage and sawed through my core. There was nothing there but light gushing out of me.

I closed my eyes as tears streamed down my cheeks and soaked my face. In a breath of a whisper, words found their way to my lips before I thought to question them. "Daddy, help me."

My eyes snapped open and I watched in awe as my pointer finger slowly extended out. If I was controlling it, I really didn't know how. The rest of my body remained paralyzed. But if this was the last chance I was going to get, I sure as heck wasn't going to waste it.

I locked my unfocused gaze on the bowl and attempted a mind push. Nothing. The blue globe began to glow bright neon blue. I fought back panic that I was too late and my powers were already gone—that didn't matter because I was nowhere near ready to give up. Evil little men only three apples high would not best me. One deep breath then I gritted my teeth and tried again. I pointed my lone working finger at the bowl and jerked it in the direction of the scepter.

The gnome gave a squeal of surprise as the bowl tore from his hands. Bowl and scepter connected in a loud crack and blinding explosion of light. I shielded my head in the crook of my arm as chunks of bronze and bits of opalescent glass showered the room.

My powers slammed back into me with the force of juiced up defibrillator paddles as the spell broke. The six-panel door splintered under Big Mike's boot as he kicked it open. Gabe and Terin followed him and rushed to my side.

Gnomes scurried and scampered to the far corner of the room. In perfect choreographed synchronization a dozen of them planted their feet while others climbed on their shoulders, then another layer, and another, until they were standing about ten gnomes high. Bernard was the cherry on top. He swung his cane over his head, uttered a few undecipherable words, and *BAM!* All the little men melted together and grew into one gigantic gnome. It filled half the room with its monstrous presence, yet still maintained the rosy cheeks and cute little upturned button nose that fooled people into finding them adorable.

"And you thought it was a stupid phobia!" I yelled at the slack jawed cavalry.

CHAPTER THIRTY-ONE

"Grab the girl! I'll get the big guy," Big Mike ripped off his black t-shirt like it was nothing more than tissue paper. The muscles of his arms bulged as he rolled his shoulders to release his wings. Reaching over his head he unsheathed the sword strapped to his back and leapt into battle. The blade whirled and twirled around him at a blinding speed.

The giant gnome raised its hand and shot a lightning bolt out of its palm aimed directly for Big Mike's heart. The fast flying blade deflected it in mid-swing and our avenger pressed on.

Terin got to work freeing me while Gabe stood guard.

"Hold still." Flame arced from her finger and slowly melted a section of the metal away. The heat blistered and scorched my skin, but it'd be far worse if I moved.

Instead, I held painfully still and muttered through clenched teeth, "Where's Kendall?" Her healing feathers sounded more appealing than a warm bubble bath.

Gabe's chest shook in a steady growl as he kept his feline eyes locked on the fight. "Sophia's death hit her hard. Kendall blames herself for running off."

My head snapped to the side so hard I scraped my cheek against the tabletop. "*What?*"

Clad only in a pair of mesh shorts, Gabe glanced my way over his bare broad shoulder. The deep lines etched into his forehead reflected his sorrow. "We lost her, Cee. I'm so sorry."

Terin finished with one cuff and rounded the table to do the other.

A pit of despair grew in my stomach and bile rose in my throat. Since all this began none of the members of my team had fallen. Sophia was the first. My friend. My co-worker. My muse.

"I should've been able to protect her," I muttered. Tears filled my eyes that I dared not spill in the middle of a battle. "She counted on me to keep her safe."

"No!" Terin snapped. Flames burned bright in the irises of her eyes, adding a supernatural intensity to her declaration. "She counted on you to *save the world*. We are at war, Conduit of the Gryphon. *Never* forget that. Do your job so her death wasn't in vain."

I wanted to have myself a nice little breakdown, but Terin was right. It needed to wait. Once we all got out of here alive I could sob and snot my brains out.

Without warning Gabe leapt over the table in a cat-like bound. He shoved Gnome-zilla away a second before it crashed down on me. Big Mike stood waiting. As soon as the gnome was back in play, he spun with the sword over his head and brought it down with enough force to sever the beast's arm. Not a drop of blood spilled, nor did Gigan-gnome cry out in pain. Instead it gave a jovial grin as the severed limb reverted back into 25 normal-sized gnomes that pounced on Big Mike in a wave of tiny boots and pointy hats.

Our rough and tumble biker dude muttered a quick, "Ah, hell," before gnomes covered him.

The little men latched on to him biting, clawing, and scratching anything—and I do mean anything—they could grasp. Big Mike knocked some off with his wings, and flung others away. Airborne gnomes emitted high-pitched *squeeee*s as they flew through the air, but they hit the ground and scurried right back to rejoin the fight.

Unfortunately, Big Mike no longer drew Big Daddy Gnome's attention away from me. He turned my way with a jolly grin that was downright terrifying.

"Cee? All those times I razzed you for being freaked out by these things?" Gabe's voice dropped to an inhumane growl as his muzzle swelled from his face. "I take it back."

Metal clanged and the cuff fell away from my wrist. I sat up and rubbed the tender flesh. Free from the shackles my speed healing was once again active. The angry red skin instantly softened to pink.

"Gabe!" Terin yelled from behind me. "Get Celeste out of here. *Now.*"

I expected Gabe to argue. He hated being sidelined for a fight. But when he glanced in Terin's direction his feline eyes widened and he hustled to usher me off the table.

"What are you doing?" I demanded as he hooked his furry arm around my waist and scooped me up. "We can't leave them here! Come on! We've gotta rally our forces and all that crap!"

"Trust me, our forces have got this." Gabe's mane twitched as he jerked his chin in Terin's direction. "We've got our own girl on fire, and I don't mean Katniss."

I whipped my head around and my jaw swung open. I'm the warrior to mankind but I suddenly felt ... insignificant. I'd gone head to head with the Titans of Fire, but even they paled in comparison to the power and elegance that Terin exuded. Her curvaceous frame raised and lengthened until she stood almost as tall as Gnome-zilla. Fiery wings grew from her arms. Flames emanated from every inch of her.

Eyes of smoldering ember blinked and focused on us. Through lips that snapped and hissed with licking flames she warned, "Now would be a good time to run."

Gabe held me tight and leapt across the room and out of the way. Terin lifted into the air with one flap of her sizzling wings and soared straight for the giant gnome. She caught it in a deadly hug and cocooned it in her embrace as her blaze flared high enough to scorch the ceiling. We saw or heard nothing within that wall of flame, but knew a terrible fate consumed Bernard and his accomplices. The gnomes attacking Big Mike immediately halted and vanished in a blink to save themselves. Big Mike swiped his sword from the ground and slid it back in its leather sheath.

Physical and emotional exhaustion took its toll. I let my head lull against Gabe's shoulder and watched as ash covered the room like a heavy snow.

CHAPTER THIRTY-TWO

Ah, life as the Conduit. One minute I'm shampooing gnome ash out of my hair, the next sliding into formal wear.

Without argument, Rowan was a *gigantic* tool, but he did have great taste in clothing. Gone was the pink monstrosity Kendall tried to force on me. It went to ugly dress heaven when the hall blew up. This soft taupe empire-waist dress was much more my style. I turned one way and then the other as I admired my reflection in the full-length mirror. The fabric of the bodice and capped sleeves was gathered. At the waist the material flowed to the floor but parted in the middle to reveal layers of airy ivory fabric beneath. A ribbon embroidered with shades of light blue, ivory, and gold around the neckline, under the bust and down the split in the material added an elegant touch.

I cocked my head to the side and traced my finger across the ribboned neckline. The gorgeous garment, straight out of the 17th century, would thrill Alaina. This was a shockingly thoughtful gesture from a sociopath whose self-serving motives were always shrouded in darkness and mystery. Rowan really was a walking question mark, and now that he had vanished without a trace he probably always would be. A knock on the door signaled the arrival of the hair and make-up team—here to transform this average looking girl into an average looking girl with flowers in her hair and more make-up on than she's comfortable wearing.

An hour later I was primped, primed, and hunkered in the gold décor bridal suite with my mom, Kendall, and Grams awaiting

Alaina's appearance and the kick-off of the wedding festivities. I peered across the room at Kendall and bit my cheek to stifle a laugh. While Kendall's dress was identical to mine that was where our similarities ended. If the hair and make-up team had been allowed entry into Keni's room she must've *severely* ticked them off somehow. Her inky black hair stuck up off her head in a mess of knots and spikes. Dramatic black eyeliner made her icy blue eyes severe and startling. The black lipstick she wore made it look like a pen exploded in her mouth. For the first time in my life I felt like the more attractive Garrett sister. I sat up a little straighter and smiled to myself.

Mom refused to accept this new 'tude of Keni's. First she tried catering to Keni's whims to snap her out of it. When that proved pointless she decided to alter her approach and attempt conversation.

"Keni, honey, are you sure there's nothing you want to talk about?" she asked for the fifth time.

"O.M.G., Mom! As if you could even comprehend the depth of my feelings!" Keni huffed and stomped across the room to brood in a corner.

"This phase is even more annoying than her *Hannah Montana* phase," I muttered after her dramatic storm off.

Mom's eyebrows and finger raised in unison. "*Nothing* is more annoying than the Hannah Montana phase."

I nodded my agreement and shuddered at the memory.

Grams sauntered in from the sitting room, carrying a giant gift bag with a three-tiered wedding cake on the side. "All the wedding gifts are in here and this one was opened … kind of. You've gotta see it." She set the bag on the end table and extracted a water pitcher in the shape of a giant rooster. "Hah! All the phallic jokes that go along with that just boggle the mind, don't they?"

Mom's nose crinkled in distaste. "That has to be a re-gift. No one would spend their money on that."

"This is *Alaina's* wedding." Kendall *tsk*ed with an exaggerated eyeroll. "She may have actually *registered* for it."

"Well, when the time comes she can just give it away," Grams said with a shrug of her black sequin clad shoulder and deposited the colorful rooster back in his bag.

The impact of those words hit me with a jolt. An echo of them rang through my mind like the faint melody of a familiar song.

When the time comes, give it away.

Cold dread tiptoed up my spine. I tried—and failed—to remember where I heard those words, but the foreboding nature of them forced me to wipe my suddenly sweaty palms on the nearest tablecloth.

A welcome distraction came when the bathroom door squeaked open and Alaina made her grand entrance. Everyone except Kendall gasped. (Apparently teenage angst prevents any and all expressions of awe or wonderment.) Her gown featured the same empire waist with the material split down the front as the bridesmaids' dresses. Rich ivory fabric flowed to the floor and extended behind her in a small train. A thick band of embroidered gold with tiny scalloped red roses capped the neckline, the end of her long, belled sleeves, and trailed along the parted fabric. A thicker band of it cinched her tiny waist. Layer after layer of antique lace peeked out from the slit in the material was layer after layer of antique lace. Her long auburn hair fell in waves down her back in a curtain made all the more lovely by the gold and diamond tiara atop her head and a veil dotted with crystals that skimmed the floor with each step.

Unlike in the bridal shop, with *this* dress she exhibited no doubt or hesitation. Her moss green eyes brimmed with glee and a rosy hue filled her cheeks. "I'm ready. Let's go get me married!"

The heels of Grams black bling-tastic mules thumped across the floor as she strode to the door and threw it open wide. "Heck yeah! My groove thang is ready to shake it up at your reception!" She shimmied her hips in a preview *no one* wanted to see.

Mom's porcelain skin turned beet red and her hand fluttered up to her mouth. "Oh my!" She glanced at the floor, ceiling, anywhere but at gyrating Grams. "Well, there *that* is."

CB ✴ ℬ

White chairs formed perfect lines on either side of the white aisle runner. At the end of the runner sat two enormous planters with sprays of bright orange flowers exploding out of them. Old fashioned light posts adorned with orange, plum, white, and yellow blooms lined the path to the altar. The ceremony that forever bound my brother to our former Spirit Guide took place under an archway that dripped with flowers of the same color scheme, ivy and other assorted greenery.

The framed picture of my father—and one Alaina added of Caleb—graced a small table next to the alter. That familiar ache returned as my gaze lingered on Caleb's gorgeous smile while I listened to Gabe and Alaina recite their vows. Happiness radiated off the couple. Love resided here today; its presence undeniable. We all served as witnesses that happy endings really do happen. Joy that my big brother found his happily ever flooded my heart. Somehow, someday I would describe this event to Caleb in precise detail. That resolute vow made to myself eased the void inside me in a truer and more real way than Rowan's power ever could.

Not a tear or quivering lip came from the bride *or* groom, exchanged blissful smiles, and spoke the words that bound their souls together forever. As soon as the minister presented them as Mr. and Mrs. Gabe and Alaina Garrett, Gabe grabbed Alaina by the waist and hoisted her to his eye level. She wrapped her arms around his thick neck and laid a huge kiss on him. The crowd went wild with applause. In true Grams fashion she rang her cowbell.

 CB ✳ BO

As I entered the tent for the reception, I struggled not to go all slack-jawed yokel. Nothing I ever envisioned compared to the opulence of a Biltmore-style backyard tent reception. Crystal chandeliers hung from the canvas ceiling. A raised dance floor lit up in rhythm to each song played sat at the far end of the tent right next to the DJ's booth. Pristine white linens covered the tables. Crystal bowls filled one quarter full with black rocks while water lilies floated on top of water that reached the bowl's rim sat perfectly positioned in the center of each table. This place was so extravagant I was afraid to touch anything for fear of bringing the whole thing tumbling down.

For safety sake I positioned myself by the hors d'oeuvre table and made it my own personal goal to see how many crab cakes I could eat before I burst. I had just mashed number fourteen in my mouth when the Grand Councilwoman strode up flanked by Big Mike and Terin.

The Grand Councilwoman spoke through pursed lips, her normal haughty air in full effect. "Sophia's funeral will be held on the Spirit Plane. You will be required to attend. At which time a new Spirit Guide will be appointed to you."

"You suck at small talk. Do you know that about yourself?" I asked and licked the flaky crumbs from my fingers.

The previous night I cried until I ran out of tears over Sophia's death. When the last of the sobs wrenched from my trembling body I stared into the night and thought about her life. As a muse she inspired others to live life to the fullest. As my friend, she wouldn't want me to mourn her. She'd want me to remember her fondly and keep living, especially since my calling came with no guarantee of a long life expectancy. In her honor, I decided to embrace life as fully as possible. Starting with reveling in a hobby I had truly come to love ... harassing the Grand Councilwoman. Making her squirm brought me great joy.

She squinted as though she either didn't get my humor or wanted to pinch my head off, hard to tell which.

"Is Alaina going to be reinstated?"

A hint of a smile twitched at the corners of Big Mike's mouth.

The Grand Councilwoman clasped her hands behind her back and peered around at the mingling guests. "The opportunity was offered to her. She turned it down. Apparently she has decided mortality is a good fit for her. The Council must now gather to discuss who to appoint."

I wiped my hands on a napkin and flashed my best, most innocent smile. "Could I cast my vote for anyone that is *not* a creepy, berry-addicted gnome that's crossed over to the dark side?"

She cleared her throat and tried to look unaffected. Her feathers may have been hidden, but I still managed to ruffle them. "Yes. Well, in case I failed to say it before ... "

"You did," Terin interjected and shot me a wink.

I pressed my lips together to squash a threatening snicker.

The Grand Councilwoman glared Terin's way before she continued. "I am deeply sorry the guide I assigned tried to terminate you and therein destroy the world."

"These things happen, right?" I chucked her shoulder with the inside of my fist. A horrified look crossed her face at the casual nature of my touch. Judge me if you will, but that just made it funnier. "Maybe in the future you could try a more thorough screening process? Google them. I hear that's *really* effective."

"Goo ... *what*? I shall do no such thing to them!" Her chalk white complexion turned a deeper shade of crimson by the second. "Michael, please escort me to my room. This human disguise is becoming increasingly difficult to maintain under these deplorable conditions!"

I gave her a little wave goodbye as Big Mike offered her his arm. His muscles visibly bulged even through his tux. He gave a brief nod in my direction and led Her Grand Snootiness out. Terin lingered behind, her bright red-hair set ablaze—figuratively—by the golden jersey dress that skimmed over the curves of her body.

We exchanged uncomfortable smiles as the wedding guests banged their butter knives against their glasses to prompt the bride and groom to engage in yet another movie screen worthy smooch.

"So … what are you?" I asked in my best attempt at casual.

A curtain of red hair brushed her shoulder when she turned my way; her face an unreadable mask. "I'm your cautionary tale."

"My what now?"

She plucked a glass of champagne from a passing caterer and raised it to her lips. Even after her sip she paused and ran her finger along the rim of the flute before speaking. "Did they warn you that you could lose your humanity as the Conduit of the Gryphon?"

Alaina told me that shortly after I learned of my calling. Right around the time I learned that the Gryphon could read my mind and that's how he knew when to zap me with a new power or ability. At one time these things had worried me to no end. I'd all but forgotten about both in the craziness that followed.

"Yes." The satin ribbon that hung down from the wreath of flowers in my hair tickled my neck as I nodded.

"That's what happened to me." Her words hung heavy in the air between us. I half expected them to fall to the ground with a thud.

"You're a Conduit? Of the Gryphon?" My voice rose with accusation. Sure, it was stupid to feel the Gryphon was somehow cheating on me but still …

"Heavens, no," she scoffed with an arrogant smirk I found borderline insulting. (All the while being relieved the Gryphon and I remained exclusive.) "I'm the Conduit of the Phoenix. A girl chosen, just as you were. I fought many battles and with each a bit more power was given to me. In the midst of a fight that almost killed me I embraced the powers of the Phoenix completely. A voluntary choice I have regretted every day since. Because that's the day I gave up my mortality."

I squinted at her as if the truth would reveal itself in some visible display right then. "But ... you look so *normal*. You know—when you're not flying through the air on fire."

Her laugh held more sadness than humor. "I may look it, but the changes I have undergone have made it impossible to live on this plane of existence. My oddities would be too easily noticed among mortals. Since that day, and for every day until the end of time, my home will be the Spirit Plane."

I snagged a soda from a passing tray and drain it in one gulp as the severe implication of her words registered in my brain. "So to summarize," I wiped my lips on the back of my hand, "proceed with caution?"

Her gaze locked on mine. A small flame flickered in the center of her pupils. "Proceed with *utmost* caution."

I took a deep breath and exhaled through my nose, all the while nodding like an idiot. "In the last twenty four hours you've saved my life and then scared the living hell out of me. I think I need to talk to other—less intense—people for a while."

"Completely justified. I'll be seeing you, Gryphon girl."

"Probably sooner than I'd like, Phoenix."

A flip of her thick red waves and she sashayed off into the crowd, catching the attention of every guy she passed.

"I gotta learn to walk like that," I muttered, and made my best attempt as I returned to my seat at the bridal table.

Mom caught my arm halfway there. "If you're looking for the nearest bathroom, sweetie, it's out the back and across the lawn to the Carriage House. Can't miss it."

Shot for sexy saunter, achieved pee-pee dance. *Awesome.*

Mom squeezed my arm then went back to her conversation with her cousin whose weird name I never remembered. Tazzy? Taffy? Tappy? No matter, they weren't paying attention to me anymore anyway.

Once again walking in my normal gait, I weaved through the crowd until I found my seat and flopped down with my elbows on the table. Despite the mountain of catastrophes that had almost ruined this day, it had somehow gone off without a hitch. On the dance floor, locked in each other's arms, the bride and groom swayed to a Rascal Flatts song. Alaina wiped a bit of frosting left from them feeding each other the cake from Gabe's cheek and showed it to him. He laughed and licked it off her finger. Grams and Dr. Allyn were also on the dance floor. Her head rested on his shoulder, his hand lingered on her butt. I groaned and averted my eyes. *Gross, horny, old people.* By the bar a bunch of the football players tried to coax the bartender into handing over a pitcher of beer. The bartenders stoic, thoroughly unamused expression made it clear even from across the room that the teens would have a sober night.

Suddenly a chill tracked down my spine. I didn't see Kendall. I rose to my feet and performed another sweep of the room with a fresh sense of urgency. A familiar bad feeling sent icy prickles across the back of my neck and down my arms.

That's when I saw them. Kendall stood by the entrance. A tall, slender man with a sinister, seductive smile had his arm locked tightly around her shoulders. *Alec.* No, actually Barnabus. Really, the bad guys needed to start wearing nametags.

He dug into the inside breast pocket of his tailored tuxedo and drew something out. I saw a glint of metal and needed no further provocation. I crossed the tent in a blur of speed that blew napkins from tables and twisted my uncle's bad toupee around.

Terin made it there a second before I did and positioned her body to block my way. Alec's full lips twisted up in an amused smirk. "Easy, hot head, this has nothing to do with you."

Before I made the slightest move to prevent it—he plunged a syringe containing a milky white liquid deep into Kendall's neck. Her eyes widened. Her black painted lips formed a scream that never escaped. I charged for Alec, fully prepared to rip his throat out in front of all the wedding guests.

Terin caught me and held me back as Alec extracted the needle and pocketed it.

"No! Look!" she demanded in an urgent whisper.

Reluctantly, I paused. The warm peaches and cream hue returned to Kendall's complexion. The sparkle blinked back into her ocean blue eyes.

Alec released his hold on her and Kendall gave a wide-eyed, toothy grin. "Aw! Cee, look at you! You look so pretty! What are you all dressed up for?" She then noticed her surroundings and did a double take. "Wait ... where are we?"

My forehead creased in confusion. "Gabe and Alaina's wedding. You don't remember?"

"I missed the wedding?! But how ... " Her black painted nails started to flutter up to her mouth. She caught sight of them and froze. "What happened to me and who gave me the manicure from hell?"

"What happened is a great question," I echoed and turned my attention to my former love interest. "What did you do to her?"

"My minions told you they were trying to give the bride and groom a wedding present from me," he remarked with a casual lift of his shoulder. "That was it. Your sister was attacked by a Spider Demon at a dress shop and became infected. Her wings couldn't heal this because it was demonic poison. The venom effects emotion—causes moodiness, impulsive and rash behavior, and in her case bad decisions regarding her hair."

Kendall's hand flew to her head. Her voice rose to a high-pitched squeak of alarm. "*What's the matter with my hair?!*"

"I just injected her with an elixir that cured her of the venom." Alec's lips curled up in a malicious grin. "As you kids would say, you owe me one."

"Seriously! What the freak happened to my hair?!" Keni squawked. Her eyes darted around for a mirrored surface of any kind.

I kept my gaze locked on Alec/Barnabus. "Terin, why don't you go get my Grams and the two of you take Kendall to the restroom. Be prepared for a fashionista meltdown."

Terin hesitated, her own warrior nature kept her rooted where she stood.

"Go ahead, Phoenix," I encouraged. "He didn't come here to fight. Did you?"

"Not at all. I ask only for one dance." He offered his arm to me and gave me what he probably considered a charming grin. It missed the mark and came across as skeevy.

Reluctantly, Terin led Keni away. Gabe pulled away from his bride. His lip curled up in a snarl and his wide back rounded. I refused to let their perfect day suffer even a slight disaster. Even if it meant doing the unspeakable …

I held up a hand to reassure Gabe. "One dance. Then you leave and don't come back."

"You have my word," he vowed with a formal bow, then offered his arm to me once more.

Wrong and unnatural is the only way to describe how it felt to link my arm with his and let him lead me to the dance floor. As soon as I stepped onto the glowing floor he twirled me into a classic ballroom dancing stance and waltzed me around the floor with his hand on the small of my back.

I gave a muddled squeak of protest and tried to keep up.

"There was a time you would've loved to get lost in my arms." He grinned.

"There was a time when you didn't overuse hair products. Things change."

His pungent aftershave assaulted my nostrils as he leaned in to whisper, "I've always appreciated your sharp tongue, girl."

"And I appreciated burying one of your own talons deep into your chest." I pulled back and searched the planes of his face for traces of my long lost friend. "Tell me, how did you weasel your way into Alec's body anyway?"

Pride straightened his spine and oozed from his smirk. "I told you once that I had tricks, girl. You destroyed my body, but left a perfectly good—if slightly bloody—one lying right outside the door. Settling my spirit into him was easy enough considering you practically gift wrapped him for me."

I hated to ask this question but had to know. "Is ... is he still in there somewhere?"

"Oh, he's here." He nodded and twirled me around like a rag doll. "Buried deep. He rarely fights to the surface like he used to. You know, I think you may have broken his heart that day in the hospital when he *pleaded* for your help."

I jerked out of his arms. My hands balled into fists so tightly my nails sliced into my palms. "Shut up. Don't you dare ... "

"Tsk, tsk, tsk." Barnabus waved his finger side-to-side then caught me by the waist and pulled me back to him. "I didn't come here to fight. If I *had* I wouldn't have saved your sister."

"Why did you come here?" I asked and fought the urge to close my eyes as he spun me in yet another dizzying turn.

"A demonic war is coming. Surely, you know that." He gave a nod and a wink to Gabe when we waltzed past him and Alaina. My brother's chest puffed up and a faint growl rumbled past his lips.

"One *you're* starting with all your newly formed minions. How many innocent people have you stolen from their lives to turn into your slaves?"

"I gave their pointless lives meaning!" For a second his cool façade faltered and rage broke through. As quick as it came on, he blinked it away. His smile—as smooth and deadly as the blade of a sword—returned. "I have a score to settle with the Countess. She set me up and got me killed. For that she *will* pay."

"She wants *you* dead, you want *her* dead, and I want you *both* dead. You two kill each other and I'm off the hook for this whole Conduit business. That being said, I gotta know, why tell me this? What does any of it have to do with me?"

He peered at me with intensity in his cobalt eyes that bordered on psychotic. "Because I want you to fight by my side."

I snorted a loud, rather unfeminine laugh. "I'm sorry, *what*? You're kidding right?"

"No, my dear. I'm deadly serious."

"And what makes you think I would *ever* do that?"

Barnabus stopped dancing and leaned in close enough for his cheek to graze mine. His hot breath warmed my neck as he whispered, "Because … I can give you your boyfriend back."

About the Author

Stacey Rourke lives in Michigan with her husband, two beautiful daughters, and two giant, drooly dogs. She loves to travel, has an unhealthy shoe obsession and an unjustifiable fear of garden gnomes she tried to overcome by putting one in this book. It didn't work. She is currently hard at work on the continuations of the Gryphon series, as well as other literary projects.

Visit her at www.staceyrourke.com

Facebook at http://www.facebook.com/pages/Stacey-Rourke/

or on Twitter @Rourkewrites

Catch up on all the Garrett gang's adventures!

The Sidekick Chronicles Volume II: A Pirate's Tale
and
The Final Gryphon Series Novel, Ascension
Coming Soon!

CPSIA information can be obtained at www.ICGtesting.com
Printed in the USA
BVOW040332051212

307247BV00007B/148/P